ICE-COLD DEATH

OONA GOODLIGHT, BOOK ONE

ALEXES RAZEVICH

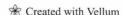

*B*rad Keel was deader than dead.

He lay on the ice rink, his blank eyes staring at the wooden beamed ceiling, his hands clutched around the broken hockey stick jutting from his gut. It wasn't the stick that killed him though. Most likely death had come from the nasty gash across his throat.

Blood had gushed from the wound, spraying out and pooling to either side of his body. It could have been cut by a dull knife, that ragged gash, but my bet was on the blade of an ice hockey skate. It was an ugly way to die.

"Man," Tosh, our team captain, said. All his shock and horror lay exposed in that one word.

He and some guy I didn't know stood near me by the glass wall that surrounded the small ice rink. Behind us, in the dressing area, my teammates sat on long, scarred wooden benches or stood, arms folded across their bodies, some leaning against a bank of gray metal lockers on the back wall. Hockey bags lay scattered at their feet.

"Man," Tosh said again. "Someone was pissed as fuck at Brad."

I exhaled a long slow breath. He wasn't wrong.

I cast my senses out but there was no trace of who had done this—no lingering anger so potent I could chase it to its source, no traceable guilt or regret, no psychic scent left behind.

Joe Lopez, who ran the Zamboni and had opened the rink for us at 5:30 this morning, was on his cell to 911. I heard him giving vague details—"No, a team had booked the ice for an early morning practice is all. We found the body together, at the same time. Yes. No." His voice shook. His hand holding the cell phone shook.

He gave the rink location, pressed the call off, and stowed his phone in one of the pockets of his dark-green cargo shorts.

The sudden silence—broken only by the occasional cough or shuffling of a hockey bag—was downright eerie inside a darkened shopping mall, the small ice rink the only area lit. I looked across the ice to the glass tables and wire back chairs on the far side where fans and family could sit. Beyond them was a restaurant, closed now, that did a good business with kids' skating birthday parties and shoppers. To my left were the usual retail stores you'd expect, though I couldn't make out the names in the gloom.

Finally, Tosh said, "I guess we're not getting any ice time in this morning."

A couple of the guys said, "No," or "Doesn't look like it," but mostly people only talked in low tones to the person next to them, all of us wondering what came next.

The team had shown up at this ungodly early hour for a between-seasons practice. The Rink Rats were a stable team with very little turnover. We'd all known each other for years and the guys more or less accepted me, the only woman on the team in a sport that was definitely male dominated, as just another skater.

The only stranger was a guy who looked to be a few years older than me—I guessed twenty-seven, twenty-eight at a stretch—who'd come to substitute in net since our regular goalie was on his honeymoon.

I kept my thoughts to myself. Even with no psychic fingerprints on the murdered man, the violence and death vibe swirling around was making my head ache and my stomach cramp. There's lots of upside to being psychic and an empath, but there's equal downsides. Feeling Brad Keel's surprise turn to fear and then to pain as he was murdered wasn't something I could talk to the guys about. They'd think I was nuts.

Vertigo hit me suddenly and hard. I swayed on my feet. The substitute goalie, the one person I didn't already know, grabbed my shoulders to steady me. The instant his hands closed on my shoulders, I felt the magic pulsing through him. I probably would have felt it earlier if seeing Brad's body hadn't sucked up all my attention.

"You're a wizard?" I muttered as he gently moved me to one of the small wooden benches the rink provided instead of locker rooms.

I felt him stiffen ever so slightly as he eased me onto the bench. No one watching would have noticed, but I felt it. So, the answer was yes.

I sank down on the bench.

Tosh took a step toward me. "Hey, Oona. You okay?"

I waved him off with a small hand gesture.

The stranger-goalie was hunkered down over his heels next to me. "You sure you're okay? You look pale."

I nodded, but I wasn't okay. The vertigo was overwhelming. Visions of the murder flooded my mind.

3

The clock read three thirteen. The night sky outside was cloudy and charcoal gray. A small breeze blew. Brad was laughing as his companion unlocked the mall's door. Both men had ice skates slung over their shoulders and hockey sticks in their hands but weren't carrying bags—so they hadn't brought the rest of the usual equipment. They stepped inside the dark building. Brad's companion flipped on the light over the rink.

I sniffed and smelled the marijuana they'd smoked earlier. Both were still feeling the effects.

And then they were on the small rink, skating hard against each other, the way friendly rivals do. I couldn't see a face for Brad's companion, but there was something off about him—a weird sort of doubling—as though he were out of phase with himself. His aura was doubled, too, somehow, the muddy forest green of jealousy and resentment overlaid with an oscillating black of non-forgiveness. One person could show both, but something felt twinned about this guy, as if his dark emotions weren't his alone.

I felt his fury growing stronger as they skated. There was history between these two, history Brad wanted to put aside. His companion reveled in his anger, stoked it with harsh memories I couldn't catch hold of enough to know their source.

The companion stole the puck from Brad and laughed cold and hard. Annoyed, Brad hacked hard at the other man's stick, breaking it three-quarters of the way down the shaft. The shaft broke unevenly, leaving a sharp jagged point on one side of the break.

His companion's fury rose but he hid it, laughing, skating backward, taunting Brad by waving his broken stick like a sword. Brad followed, skating forward, laughing at his friend's antics until the companion had maneuvered them into

4

the faceoff circle at center ice. The companion stopped then, digging his skate blades into the ice, bending his knees, setting his balance.

Brad stopped only inches away.

"Sorry about your stick, bro," Brad said.

The other man lifted the broken shaft and held it in front of his chest, horizontally in both hands. With a grunt, he shoved the stick hard against Brad's chest. At the same moment, he swung his right leg around and tripped Brad to the ice.

"What the hell?" Brad shouted and planted his hands on the ice to lever himself up.

Before he could, the companion plunged the pointed end of the broken stick into Brad's gut. Brad grabbed the stick with both hands and tried to pull it free. It was jammed in too deeply and he couldn't move it. Blood leaked from the wound.

"Help," Brad said, his voice cracking.

The companion stood a moment, staring down at his struggling friend. He skated up toward Brad's head, lifted his foot and ran his skate blade hard over Brad's neck.

Blood spurted from the wound, the spray jetting out across the ice. Brad's mouth dropped open. Stunned. He kept trying to pull the stick from his chest even as blood was pouring from his neck, his life leaking away.

His hands on his hips, the companion watched the seconds it took Brad to lapse into unconsciousness, then calmly exited the ice and sat down on a bench.

I had that odd out of phase sense again, as if I saw him out of focus and doubled. I struggled to see his face but couldn't get a fix on it. He took off his skates, put on his running shoes, and walked out of the mall, turning off the lights and locking the door behind him.

On the rink, Brad was already dead.

I shivered, disgusted to realize that I sat only inches away from where the killer had calmly removed his skates and left Brad to bleed out on the ice. I scooted away to the other end of the bench.

My team stood around me, concern written on their faces. The sub-goalie/wizard held out a cup of water. I didn't know where it had come from but was grateful for it.

The goalie said softly, "You screamed."

My face grew hot. I'm the only woman on an ice hockey team with fourteen guys—and I'd screamed like a little girl.

The paramedics arrived with a stretcher. Through the large glass doors that faced the street, I saw three big, red fire trucks, an ambulance, and a police car. Two cops followed in behind the paramedics. The cops took one look at all of us gathered there and frowned ever so slightly.

"They'll split us up for the interviews," the substitute goalie said. His voice was a near whisper, speaking only to me.

"You've been through this before?"

He shook his head slightly. "Heard about it from clients."

I wanted to know what kind of work he did that people described being interviewed by the police to him. Before I could ask, the shorter of the two cops—his name tag read R. Scott—said, "Is someone in charge of this group?"

The taller, heavier cop stepped away and pulled out his phone. He spoke too quietly for me to hear what he was saying.

Most everyone, myself included, looked at Tosh, who shrugged and said, "I'm the team captain."

"Good," Officer Scott said. "We're calling to have some people come in to help with taking statements. In the meantime, we'll start speaking with everyone one at a time. What I need you to do," he made clear eye contact with Tosh, "is keep those who haven't been interviewed yet from discussing what happened among themselves. Can you do that?"

Tosh nodded.

Officer Scott flashed a thin but approving smile. "Can you tell me why you are all here?"

Tosh glanced at the knot we'd formed, the team unconsciously coming together to support each other.

"We came for an early practice."

Scott wrote in a notebook he carried.

Why a paper notebook, I wondered. Why not his phone or a tablet?

"Was the door open or did you have a key?" Officer Scott said.

Tosh looked at Joe. "He let us in."

Scott shifted his gaze. "And you are?"

"Joe. Uh, Lopez. I drive the Zamboni, keep the place clean, score keep sometimes, help out with rental skates, that sort of thing."

Scott nodded and made another scribbling motion in his notepad. "Was the door locked or open?"

"Locked," Joe said. "It's a habit I have, to always try the door before I unlock it. A couple of times kids have broken in and stolen stuff from over there." He jutted his chin toward the restaurant, protected now by a pull-down metal grate. "I like to be sure no one has gotten inside before me and might still be here."

The officer nodded and turned back to Tosh. "Go on."

Tosh hiked up his shoulders. "We walked in and saw Brad dead on the ice."

Scott didn't show any outward change, but I felt his interest climb. He motioned with his head for Tosh to follow him and led Tosh around the edge of the rink until they stood near the door we'd come in that morning.

7

I strained to hear, but they were too far away. I really wanted to hear that conversation.

From the corner of my eye, I saw the substitute goalie/wizard muttering to himself. There was a sudden pop in my ears and I heard Tosh and Officer Scott as clearly as if they stood next to me. I shot the wizard a Thank You nod, acknowledging that I'd felt his magic and appreciated him sharing so I could hear what Tosh and the policeman were saying.

"You knew the victim?" Scott asked.

"Hockey is a small world. Most of us know each other. Brad played a division up but subbed down occasionally. He subbed for our team over at Bay Harbor, the ice rink on Western, a couple of times last season."

Scott glanced back our way, his eye catching on me for some reason. I looked away.

"So, you all knew him?" Scott said.

Tosh nodded. "Casually. I don't think any of us knew him well."

My head rang with pain like an anvil being pummeled by a sledgehammer. Leftover tension from the vision. Or maybe an effect of the magic the wizard had sent my way. Or plain old stress. I had some prescription Norco in my purse. Vicious headaches accompanied or followed my visions often enough that I needed something to let me function until they passed. I really wanted to get up and take one.

The paramedics were on the ice with the body—easier to think of it that way—the body—than as Brad. More people were arriving. I was relieved when Tosh, Officer Scott, and two more cops walked back to us.

"Detectives Smith and Bronson," Scott said, looking in turn to each of the two new cops, "will take your statements individually and then you are free to leave."

Me first, I wanted to shout. The pounding in my head was growing more painful by the moment. I couldn't get out of the rink fast enough to suit me.

I wasn't in the first group taken aside. The wizard wasn't either. He slid up next to me.

"You look like you're not feeling well."

I crossed my arms over my chest and rubbed my upper arms.

"I'm fine. Thanks for asking." I dropped my voice low. "And thanks for that enhanced hearing."

He smiled, closed mouth, and his eyes were bright. "No problem."

"Did you listen to their conversation, too?"

"Yeah."

"I'm Oona," I said.

"Diego."

We sat together a while in silence until I said, "You seem familiar. Have we met before?"

"You seem familiar to me as well," he said, "but I'm pretty sure we haven't met. I'd remember someone named Oona. Maybe we saw each other around various rinks."

"That's probably it," I said, but it didn't feel right. "Maybe grammar school or something. Did you grow up around here?"

He shook his head. "Palo Alto."

One of the detectives—Bronson, by his name tag— squatted by the bench where I sat and said, "Would you mind coming with me? We'll do your interview now."

I followed him off to a quiet spot and answered his questions the best I could. I didn't tell him about my vision of the murder.

2

*B*y the time the cops were done with me, the sun was fully up. I lugged my bag and stick back to my car parked on a side road next to the mall. I was closing my car's trunk, having stowed away my gear, when Diego walked up. The Norco had kicked in and my headache was fading. I was still shaken though. I'd never seen a dead body before, much less the dead body of someone I knew who'd been brutally killed. I felt foggy and cranky and not in the mood to talk to anyone, now that escape seemed so near.

He touched my elbow. "How are you doing?"

I pulled my arm tight to my body.

I don't like touching strangers or strangers touching me. Sometimes it was fine, and I didn't feel a thing. Sometimes I felt too much. Who wants to shake hands or even bump shoulders with someone and suddenly know exactly how miserable, or angry, or resentful they were? Strangers should keep their inner lives to themselves as far as I was concerned.

And sure, he'd already touched me when he thought I was going to faint, and all I'd felt from him then was his magic, but you never knew what you'd get when someone made physical contact.

I'd met a few wizards before, but most had been older, and frankly, rather crotchety. This Diego guy didn't feel sour or prickly at all. What he felt was no nonsense. Kind, unless you messed with him—then it would be no mercy. Goalies, in general, could be like that. Maybe wizards, too.

I felt him looking me over, his eyes flickering up and down my body. I didn't mind. Was a little flattered, in fact. It had been a while since a man looked at me that way.

He took in my physical aspects as if he were seeing me for the first time—a bit taller than average and thinnish. Brown hair pulled into a low braid to fit under my helmet, hazel eyes. I wasn't a great classical beauty, but little children didn't run away screaming when they saw me. I didn't feel any boy/girl interest toward me from him, which was okay. Preferable, in fact.

"Do you mind if I ask," he said, "what you saw when you spaced out?"

I shifted my gaze away from him for a moment. I didn't like that he knew—or seemed to know—that I'd seen *something*.

"Did you know Brad Keel?" I said, sidestepping his question. "More than casually?"

Diego nodded. "He interned for a while where I work. His father is an old friend of my boss."

"Oh," I said. "I'm sorry."

"We weren't friends," he said. "I knew him from work and I'd see him around the rink, but it was just a nod and say hi kind of thing." He shifted his weight. "So, will you tell me what happened to you in there?"

"Happened?" I said, putting all the innocence I could muster into the word.

"Yeah," he said. "Something obviously happened. There was a lot more than my magic pinballing around that rink, and it came from you."

I looked away and rubbed my thigh, thinking. Maybe it would be good to tell him. Maybe saying the words would get the pictures out of my head.

"I saw the murder. It was ugly. I didn't see who did it."

Diego nodded, taking that in. "Psychic?"

I gave a little shrug of admission.

"And empathic," he said, "judging by your physical reaction in there."

I tilted my head slightly in admission.

"Yeah," he said, and was somber a moment. His face brightened. "Would you like to get some breakfast? I'm famished."

I was all for changing the subject, too. "Will you tell me something in return?"

"Sure," he said.

"When you're in net, do you use magic to cheat?"

"Are you questioning my character?" There was no hint of insult in his voice, only bemusement.

"Just curious."

"No." He fished out his keys. "I don't need magic to win."

The way he said it, it wasn't a brag, only a statement of fact.

I raised my eyebrows, not quite believing him. "Not even in a championship game, score tied in the last minutes, the other team on a breakaway with their best shooter bearing down on you. When he shoots, you know you've misjudged and that without magic the puck is going to find the back of the net and your team will lose the game?"

He beeped his car door open. "Not even then."

I sent my senses out looking for unwarranted pride or general full-of-him-selfness, and didn't feel any of that. Didn't feel a ton of ego either. Either this Diego guy was telling the truth, or he was one of those people who so believed whatever lie they told that it sounded, smelled, and tasted like truth when they said it.

So, a saint or a sociopath?

I didn't want to have breakfast with either, or with anyone right now. The vision of what I'd seen on the rink flooded back. My knees felt too weak to hold me upright. I leaned against my car.

"I think this. . ." I said. "Brad's death. It's a bit too much."

"And you'd like to just go home."

"I would. Yes," I said. "Thanks for the offer though."

He nodded. "I'm happy to just go home myself. Things like this morning take a while to process."

"A wizard and a gentleman." I decided he probably wasn't a sociopath at least. "It was nice meeting you, even if the circumstance was pretty awful."

He grimaced. "About that wizard thing. Let's keep it between ourselves."

"Sure" I said, "so long as you don't go telling people I psychically saw the murder."

"Deal."

His gaze flickered over me again. "On the rink, do you ever use your psychic powers to know what your opponent plans to do next?"

I beeped my car door open and pulled it wide.

"I'm no saint."

My thoughts were still on Brad as I drove toward home. At 7:30 on a Sunday morning, I had the road mostly to myself. I couldn't shake thinking about Brad and his companion, his murderer, and how there was something wrong in the way I saw the killer's physical body and aura.

I drove safely, though—stopping at red lights, not running into the back of the car ahead of me. If we knew how many drivers on the road were in a *'mind somewhere else'* state at any given time, we'd never leave our houses.

I must have blanked out for a moment though, because out of nowhere a man stood in the road directly ahead of me. I pressed the brake pedal, glanced in my rearview mirror and then from side to side. A Toyota Corolla was coming up fast on my left. I couldn't change lanes to avoid the man. I couldn't swerve right up onto the sidewalk or I'd hit a woman walking a French bulldog and a German shepherd.

Why didn't the man move?

I hit my horn. The man put his hand up in a 'stop' gesture, but I couldn't stop. Not in time. I was going to hit him.

Move, dammit, I willed in his direction. But he stood rooted.

My hand on the wheel was gripped so tightly it hurt. I kept applying the brakes and using the horn. I'd hit the man, but if I could slow the car enough, maybe I wouldn't kill or badly injure him.

He still didn't move. Impact was inevitable. I closed my eyes. I didn't want to see the collision, steel on flesh.

My car passed straight through where the man had stood without so much as a gentle bump. A glance in my rearview mirror showed nothing but the back of the woman calmly walking the dogs.

14

My heart thundered in my chest. There had been a man in the road, I was sure of that. I hadn't hallucinated him.

Or maybe I had. The apparition I'd seen was the same height and body shape as Brad's murderer. Sometimes our minds play tricks.

I hung out at home until Wednesday—reading, binge-watching Netflix, attempting new recipes—trying to pretend I wasn't completely freaked out over Brad's murder. That the images didn't come flooding back at the most unexpected times. That the whole thing made me a little afraid to be outside. Better to stay in my house where I knew I was safe.

Lucky for me, I'd had canny ancestors. My great-great-grandfather, Charles Goodlight, had invested heavily in real estate in downtown Los Angeles and here in Hermosa Beach, where I lived in the house he'd built in 1914. My upstairs bedroom had a lovely sand and ocean view.

Over the years, some of the land and buildings had been sold off, but more had been bought—the Goodlights down through the generations had sharp eyes for good investments. I'd never needed to work to support myself and didn't have a job now—no unsympathetic employer demanding I show up or be fired while I sorted through my feelings about what had happened.

I'd held jobs in the past, out of sheer boredom and an abhorrence of indolence. I had a degree in English Lit and worked in preproduction for one of the studios for a while. Spending your days in a place full of egos, insecurities, and desperate wants is no job for an empathic psychic. When I found myself wondering if lining a hat with tinfoil might really work as a defense against the daily pokes and prods of my coworkers' desires, jealousies, and disappointments, I knew it was time to move on.

I'd volunteered as a dog walker at a local shelter after that. The dogs were happy to see me and didn't want anything more than to get out of their cages, but even feeling their desperation got to be too much.

These days I lived off the income from the rentals and mostly stayed home.

But really, three days brooding over Brad's murder and the awful knowledge that his killer was out there was enough. When staying indoors forever starts to seem like a good idea, it's time to get dressed and go into the world.

I'd pulled on black jeans and a white T-shirt, and was tying my red high-top sneakers, when someone knocked at the door. I looked up, surprised. I wasn't a social person. None of the people from the studio or the dog shelter had ever been to my house. I didn't keep in touch with more than a handful of people from high school and college. The place next door was a rental with a rotating cast of frat boys and surfers who I never bothered to meet. We didn't get door-to-door salespeople or Jehovah's Witnesses here on the Strand—the concrete promenade between the row of expensive ocean-front houses and the sand. I had no idea who it could be.

I debated ignoring the knock, but since I was determined to be back in the world today anyway, I figured why not go see who it was?

I opened the front door to find the wizard/goalie from Sunday standing on my wide wooden porch. I tried to remember his name, but it'd gone.

He wore shorts, a blue T-shirt, and black flip-flops. Sunday morning he'd worn a long-sleeved shirt and jeans that had hidden the tattoos that decorated both arms shoulder to wrist and the ones circling his left leg just above the ankle. I knew enough to recognize the ink as runes and signs, but not enough to know what they meant.

But what struck me most was how magic danced around his being like his own personal aurora borealis. How could I have missed that before?

"Hi," I said.

"Hi," he said back. "Do you remember me? Diego Adair. From Sunday."

"Yes, of course."

Now that I wasn't half in shock from seeing someone I knew dead in the middle of an ice rink, I was a little taken aback at how good-looking the man was. Six feet tall or there about. Dark hair just long and wild enough to give him a rakish, pirate vibe. A close-cut beard. Blue-gray eyes. Thin but built, the kind of body that might be used to display an expensive men's suit. Maybe his face was a little too craggy for everyone's taste, but I found it pleasant.

"Can I help you?" I said.

"I hope so." His gaze flicked past me into the house.

My home is my sanctuary. I really don't like having strangers invade it, but my mother didn't raise me to be rude.

"Would you like to come in?" I said.

"Thanks," he said and smiled.

I turned, and he followed me down the foyer and into the parlor. Most people would call it the living room, but it was called a parlor when great-great-grandfather had built the house and that was how I thought of it. This room had originally been much smaller, but my grandmother had knocked down the wall between the old parlor and formal dining room, making the new parlor a large, airy space.

I followed my guest's gaze, taking in the furnishings—

taupe couch and loveseat. Two blue club chairs. Teak coffee table and a teak end table at each end of the couch.

The walls were painted French blue. A large bay window with a family-antique chaise in the bay that looked out onto the Strand. I read and people-watched a lot there. Framed on one wall were the original plans for the house and a dozen family photos stretching from 1900 to the present. Other walls held paintings that had come down through the family and one or two or my own. It was a peaceful room. I liked it.

I motioned to the sofa for him to sit. I took a chair facing it.

"How can I help?" I said.

He seemed uncomfortable and didn't immediately say anything. The silence stretched out.

"Just because I'm psychic," I said, trying to lighten the mood, "doesn't mean I can read your mind and know why you've come."

He shook his head. "Sorry. Do you remember I told you that Brad had interned at my office and his father was a friend of my boss?"

I nodded.

"Brad's father has asked my boss, Tyron Danyon, to help find who killed his son. To augment the police search."

"Why would he ask that?"

He hiked up one shoulder in a half shrug. "The company, Danyon and Peet, is a private investigation firm. It's the sort of thing we do."

I filed that away: goalie, wizard, and private investigator. An unusual trio of skills.

"The police took my statement that morning at the rink," I said. "I don't know what else I could tell you that would help."

He nodded. "I would like to get a statement from you as well, but I'm here to ask for something else."

"Oh?"

"I know we said we'd keep the wizard and the psychic thing just between us, but it came out in conversation with Tyron. He'd like you to join the investigation as a psychic consultant."

I glared at him. "I don't think so."

"Can I ask why not?" Diego's voice was low, soothing. He leaned forward, his hands between his knees.

I regarded him a moment, deciding between being polite and being honest. I went for honesty.

"You broke your word about keeping my psychic abilities and what I'd seen at the rink secret. You breached a confidence and my privacy. That's not the sort of person I want to work with."

His lips drew together but he nodded. "I did, and I apologize. You don't know me, so you can't know that breaking my word wasn't done easily."

I *felt* genuine remorse from him.

"Then why did you do it?"

He sat up straight. "A couple of reasons. I knew Brad and want to find his killer. I think you can help with that. Also, to not say what you'd seen would have been holding back significant information. I couldn't do that."

He'd weighed keeping my confidence against finding a killer and chosen what seemed most important. Was most important. And yet it irked me. It took me a moment to let that go.

"I understand," I said. "Apology accepted."

A hopeful smile crossed his mouth. "Will you help?"

I put my hands on my hips and stretched my back, which suddenly felt tight. "I'm not sure I can."

I couldn't run my empathic psychic receiver all day, every day—not even 9 to 5, five days a week. It would exhaust me.

Anyway, it wasn't like I walked down the street and clearly picked up the thoughts of every person passing by. I *felt* people I knew much more than strangers. Thank God for that. Who'd want to know the mundane, profane, or even the profound thoughts, memories, hopes of every single person around? Not me. It was bad enough that I caught random thoughts and emotions whether I wanted to or not. I certainly didn't want to go looking for them.

I can read minds, but I needed to focus on the person I was reading and want to know what they're thinking. Sure, random stuff came through—a person's stray thoughts hitting me like they were speaking in my ear—but fortunately I usually had to intentionally seek a person's thoughts. The cacophony would likely drive me insane otherwise.

Knowledge could come unbidden, of course—full-blown visions, or sudden information about, and awareness of, things, people, or events that there was no normal way I could have known. Like Brad's murder.

Throwing in on the investigation would probably mean summoning up that memory more times than I would like, searching it for clues, dissecting every nuance between Brad and his killer. I shivered at the thought.

There were plenty of reasons not to take this on. I couldn't think of one reason why I should, other than basic human kindness toward Brad's family.

"Oona?" Diego said softly, some worry in his tone.

I snapped my gaze to him. "I don't think I can be of any help with this. My own abilities—"

"Magic," he said.

"What?"

"Your own magic, which is what your psychic abilities

are—inborn magic that can be trained and honed like any other skill. The more you do it, the better you'll be at it. No different than playing hockey."

I opened my mouth to speak and then closed it. I'd read my great-grandmother Cassie's diaries. She'd regarded her and her mother's abilities as magic and had trained to strengthen what she'd come by naturally. My psychic abilities were definitely inborn, and maybe I could make them stronger and more reliable, but I still wasn't going to be of any use to these people.

Diego leaned forward and tucked his hands between his knees again. "You've already admitted you use your magic to beat opponents on the rink. Why not use it to help put away a killer and bring some ease to Brad's family?"

Sheesh, I thought to myself, sling a little guilt my way why don'tcha?

But he had a point. If I *could* help, shouldn't I at least try? If I were a member of Brad's family and knew someone who maybe could have helped didn't—I'd be plenty pissed.

"How would I do that?" I said. "What would your boss expect of me?"

"Honestly, I don't know," he said. "If you come on board, we'll figure it out as we go." He paused. "The pay is excellent."

I looked at him blankly.

"But you don't need the money," he said. "Which is better, frankly. We'll be working closely together if you join us. I prefer to work with someone motivated by forces other than greed."

"How do you know I don't need the money?"

"Really?" he said, as though my question was so naive as to be ridiculous. "Danyon and Peet is an investigation firm.

Do you think Tyron would have sent me to ask for your help without checking you out thoroughly first?"

I narrowed my eyes. "You're one of those people who can be really annoying, aren't you?"

He flashed a cat-who-drank-the-cream smile. "Are you in?"

I didn't want to do this. I didn't want to leave Brad's family without answers, either.

I thought about that weird doubling thing I'd sensed from Brad's killer. What was that about? And what about my hallucination of the man in the middle of the street? Both things had freaked me out to the point where I hadn't left my house in three days—and I seriously disliked letting fear rule me.

I stood. "Would you excuse me a minute?"

Diego nodded, a puzzled expression on his face.

Everyone has favorite rooms in their house. I loved the parlor and the kitchen, which I'd recently had remodeled. I sat on one of the bentwood kitchen chairs and leaned on my elbows at the oak table and let my thoughts roll unbridled through my mind.

I really didn't want to do this 'help find the killer' thing. I didn't want to have Brad's death be the focus of my life. Didn't want to get involved with new people or meet Brad's family and feel their pain. I definitely didn't want the responsibility of trying to solve a murder. That's what the police were for.

I also didn't want to be a selfish bitch who wouldn't help when maybe she could.

And honestly, wasn't I already involved? I was the closest thing to a witness there seemed to be. And don't forget the man in the road who wasn't there. If he wasn't a hallucination, then the killer already had his sights on me. Finding him, making sure he was put away, was self-preservation. I was a big fan of self-preservation.

I poured a glass of water, drank it down, and went back to the parlor.

"Okay," I said. "But I really don't think I'll be of much help."

Diego stood. "Good. Thank you." He eased a business card out of a silver card carrier and handed it to me. "We like to be in the office by nine. See you tomorrow." He held out his hand.

I shook it—and again he felt warm and good to me.

What was I getting myself into here?

3

*D*anyon and Peet had offices in a two-story, yellow stucco building behind the Manhattan Beach mall. I parked in the underground lot and headed toward the stairs, still not completely convinced I wanted to help in the hunt for Brad's killer. But I'd said I would, and as my mother used to say, 'Your word is your bond.' I'd do the best I could.

I had no idea how private investigators dressed at the office. I wore my one skirt—black with a small white floral print—and a white blouse. Instead of my usual red high-tops or leather hiking boots, I'd opted for black flats.

At the top of the stairs and halfway down the corridor, I found a brown door with the brass plaque that read Danyon and Peet. No sounds came from behind the door, but likely that was by design and not because no one was inside. I drew in a breath, steeled myself, and turned the doorknob.

I'd pictured Danyon and Peet as a seedy outfit with a pair of owners trying to hold it together and one good-looking wizard doing all the errand-running, surveillance, background checks, and the like. The reality was nothing like that.

In the foyer, an attractive, red-haired woman about my

age—mid-twenties or so—sat in a silver Aeron chair swung sideways so I could see both it, and her, behind a mid-century modern-looking, curved blond wood desk. The woman wore a nice black dress with three-quarter length sleeves, fitted in the bodice but with a flaring skirt. Her black shoes had a medium heel.

She heard me enter and swung her chair to face me. "Oona Goodlight?" She stood and offered her hand. "I'm Terry Miller. Welcome to Danyon and Peet."

I cringed at the thought of shaking her hand. Maybe it would be okay if I said, "Sorry, I don't shake hands." If she was used to working with a wizard, it was likely eccentricities wouldn't surprise her. Every wizard I'd known was odd in his own way. It was my personal belief that needing to control the magic and power within them made them a little crazy.

But I was there as an empath as much as a psychic. I might as well touch her and see what I could learn. I took her hand and held it just a tad too long, but more than long enough to gather that she liked her job and was saving her money to go back to school to get a teaching degree.

"You're expected, of course," Terry said. "Let me buzz you in."

She reached under the desk. I heard a low hum and a snap, as if a lock was being undone. What was going on here that offices needed to be locked and people buzzed in?

The reception area was mid-century modern. The office I walked into was dark mahogany paneling with a heavy mahogany desk with carved legs set to face the door. A closed laptop was the only thing set on the immaculate and highly polished stretch of hardwood. Three armchairs upholstered in black leather faced the desk.

The woman behind the desk was speaking low into a cell phone. She had black, shoulder-length, expensively cut hair;

brown eyes; and a full mouth colored with blood-red lipstick. I guessed her to be in her early fifties.

I gave her a quick read. *Hands on* were her watchwords. She prided herself on never asking her employees to do anything she wouldn't do herself. She liked fieldwork, which surprised me given that she wore an expensive-looking heather-grey linen suit and red stiletto-heeled shoes.

Her judgmental tendencies and a big boatload of aggressiveness flowed out into the room as she eyed me while finishing her phone call.

She stood and extended her hand. "Juliana Peet."

I really didn't want to shake her hand. Her vibe was already buffeting me like high waves. I didn't want to touch her and discover things I might not want to know, but I couldn't very well refuse.

I took her hand, held it just long enough to be polite, and drew my hand back. Unconsciously, I wiped the hand that had touched her against my skirt and was a tad embarrassed when I realized what I'd done.

"Nice to meet you," I said.

A side door to the office opened and a man walked in.

"And my partner," Juliana said, "Tyron Danyon."

In contrast to Juliana's aggressive successful businesswoman look and demeanor, Tyron was tall and burly with an open, friendly face. His auburn hair was fading to white at the temples. He wore khaki shorts, a white T-shirt, and neon-green running shoes, giving him a bouncer-at-a-beach-bar vibe. He stood and held out his hand.

We shook hands and I felt his pride in Juliana and the agency they'd built together. I also felt his keen desire to find whoever had murdered his friend's son, and his fervent wish that I'd be of help.

I swallowed hard. Tyron had pinned his hopes on me. It was more expectation than I was comfortable with.

Juliana picked up her cell phone from the desk and hit a key. "Your new hire is here. Would you like to join us?"

Both Juliana and Tyron were thinking about Diego. I was *his* new hire? What did that mean? Whatever it meant, I wasn't sure I liked it.

Diego strode in wearing a charcoal gray three-piece suit with a black shirt and burgundy tie. Even though I'd already pegged him as a man who'd look good in a suit, it was hard to square this person with Goalie-Diego, or shorts, flip-flops, and magic runes Diego. With me, what you saw was pretty much what you got. He seemed more a chameleon. Was there a core Diego Adair hidden among the guises?

He took the third chair facing Juliana's desk, the one between Tyron and me. He didn't offer his hand but did give me a warm smile. I nodded but didn't smile back. Little Miss Professional, that's me.

Tyron cleared his throat. "Could you go over the details of what you saw that morning at the ice rink? The more details you can give, the better."

Clever, I thought. Get all the info from me upfront, before I've officially taken the job. Thank me and send me home.

I wasn't usually this cynical. I let a moment go by while I *felt* each person in the room again, looking for hidden agendas this time. There was nothing from Diego. Nothing from Tyron. But Juliana was prickly, straight up believing I was probably a phony like the other so-called psychics she'd run into, and not all that happy that Tyron wanted to bring me on board. She wasn't quite sure if she believed in his magic either, preferring to put Diego's successes down to charm and tenacity.

If it was just Juliana, I would have politely excused

myself, saying I was sorry but I couldn't help. But Tyron was desperate. And Brad's family would be desperate for some sort of truth and closure as well.

I laid out everything I'd seen of the murder, giving much more detail than I'd told Diego. Juliana had turned on the recorder in her phone and got down every word. Tyron's growing agony at hearing the story was physically painful to feel—this was exactly why I kept my abilities to myself and spent most of my time alone—but I kept going.

When I'd finished, Tyron and Diego were silent. Juliana rose and extended her hand again. I took it but dropped it as quickly as was polite. I had to stop myself from wiping her touch off on my skirt again.

"Thank you," she said. "We need some time to digest what you've told us and formulate a plan of attack to find the killer. Terry will give you the paperwork you need to fill out. We'll see you tomorrow."

And just like that, I was dismissed.

A round 5:30 my cell phone rang—a rare enough occurrence that I picked up the phone and frowned. My friends knew I hated to talk on the phone and preferred them to text. I didn't recognize the number and let it go to voice mail. I really hated telemarketers. The phone rang again almost immediately. Same number.

"Hello?" I said cautiously.

"Hi, It's Diego."

"How'd you get. . . "

Silly me. My cell number was on the paperwork I'd filled out at the office. I put a friendly smile into my voice. "Hey. What's up?"

"There's stick time at Bay Harbor in an hour. You didn't get your practice in Sunday. I thought you might like to go for a skate."

Actually, I'd love to go for a skate. Nervous energy had been boiling in me ever since Sunday morning. I needed to burn it off.

Diego hadn't shown any interest in me as a woman either Sunday or today in the office, but I *felt* that interest now. A vague lust, him wondering what it would be like. Flattering in *Thanks, but no thanks* kind of way. He wasn't going to act on it anyway. His main concern was what I could do to ease Brad's family's pain. He wasn't going to mess up whatever I might do toward that just for a quick romp.

It was the 'putting others first' thing that made me say, "Sounds good. I'll meet you there."

"I don't mind picking you up," he said.

"Thanks, but I'll drive myself."

I liked having my own transportation. It let me leave when I felt like it.

I had a thought and just couldn't stop myself from voicing it. "Can you skate or are you one of those net-only goalies."

He chuckled. "Come and see."

There were only five other people on the ice when we arrived, all clustered at one end of the rink running drills. That left a half-rink open for Diego and me—plenty of room to stretch our legs. We put our gear on in the benches where friends, family, and fans sat during games rather than using one of the locker rooms. I was used to dressing with men and slipped off my jeans without a thought. I wore black leggings underneath and pulled my padded ice pants and long socks on over them. I pulled the socks up over my knees, laced up my skates and fastened on my shin guards. Then elbow guards, and finally, a plain, blue jersey.

I didn't know why, but I often found the act of putting on my gear to be meditative. I like the ritual of it. Putting everything on in the same order each time. Lacing my skates just right. Taping on my ancient shin guards to the exact tightness I like. Pulling the jersey over my head and adjusting the sleeves free around the elbow guards. Maybe it has something to do with preparing to go into battle—some collective memory in our DNA. Maybe it's the calm before the storm of the game.

Evidently, Diego wasn't shy about dressing in public either and stripped down to boxers before putting on the rest of his skating gear. As a woman in a man's sport, I'd seen plenty of guys put their cup and jock on over their boxers. I'd seen guys put a towel over their lap and strip down to nothing underneath. Diego changing was nothing I hadn't seen before and I paid it little mind.

Well, maybe some mind. On a purely esthetic level, of course.

I strapped on my helmet, put on my gloves, and stepped out onto the ice, aware of Diego watching me, judging my skill level. I'm okay, but I'm not an elite skater by any means. I'm aggressive, can handle the puck some, and have a decent shot. I never felt like the guys on a team were carrying me, but I don't play in a high-skill division either.

I skated over to a loose puck and did my fanciest puck handling show-off moves and finished with my trick where I bounce the puck on the stick blade half a dozen times before I tossed it to Diego.

He caught the puck and proceeded to make much, much fancier moves—the kind I could only dream of pulling off myself. If he was as good in net as he was skating out, he was right that he didn't need magic to win.

I skated up next to him. "If you're done showing off, how about some passes."

"I've seen you skate now," he said with a grin. "I'm going to have to slow way down if we're going to pass the puck back and forth."

Men condescending to me on the ice usually got my back up. Why Diego's words struck me more as funny rather than offensive I'll never know. It must have been the glint in his eye.

We skated around, passing the puck between us. I wound up with the puck when we ran out of skate room and took a shot at the net, using one of my better tricks of hitting the top crossbar hard, so the iron rang like a church bell. In a game, hitting the post would break your heart since it meant you'd missed making a goal by an inch or two, but it sounded impressive when you were just fooling around.

The second time down it was Diego's turn to take the shot. He pivoted toward center ice and backhanded the puck straight into the top left corner as if it were drawn by a magnet.

"Zen shot," I said in reference to mounted archers who supposedly could hit a bull's-eye from a galloping horse while blindfolded. "There's no way you could see where that puck would go. Zen shot or luck."

He shrugged. "I saw the net before I turned. I knew where to aim. No luck involved."

"And modest, too." I headed back up the ice.

I hit the red line and my head suddenly ached like a rope was being tightened around it. My heart beat in my chest like a frightened bird. I felt faint and leaned on my stick for support.

Diego skated up beside me. "What's wrong?"

"He's here," I whispered. "Brad's killer."

Diego glanced around. A few more skaters and a goalie had joined the guys practicing at the other end of the rink. Players coming in for the first game of the day made a steady stream of people heading for the locker rooms.

"Can you pick him out?" Diego said.

I shook my head. "I feel him, but can't tell who, or where, he is."

My head pounded harder and my stomach knotted.

"Give me a minute," I said. "Let me see if I can home in on him."

The pain in my head intensified as I focused on trying to find the source of my discomfort. My throat went dry. I could hardly speak but managed to croak out the impressions flooding my mind.

"Something's off with this guy. I can't get a firm grip on him. But there's evil in his vibe. Nasty, vicious evil."

Diego took my elbow in his hand and steered me toward the door to leave the ice. "We're going to head out now. If the killer is a sorcerer or something else, we don't want him to realize we're here."

"No," I said. "I want to pick him out of the crowd."

Diego stopped hustling me off the ice and seemed to consider for a moment. "Okay. Give it a try."

My knees had gone weak and nausea was threatening to overtake me, but I sent my senses out and tried to identify the person emanating the cruel vibe I felt. I couldn't separate him from the other people in the rink. Dammit. I wanted to find this guy, but knew, here and now, it was a useless search. Frustration made my head hurt more. My stomach knotted and turned over.

"I need to get off the ice," I said, my voice a whisper.

I barely managed to get my skates off and my shoes on before I ran for the lady's and threw up.

4

---

*D*iego stood on my porch, the Strand and sand stretching behind him, his hands shoved into the pockets of his jeans.

"Look," he said, "It's pretty stupid if you happen to know a wizard to not take advantage of it. If you picked up the killer's vibe and he's both strange and evil, there's some chance he picked up on you, too. Let me put some protective wards on your house to keep out any bad guys."

My throat went dry. It hadn't occurred to me that the killer might have singled me out in much the same way I tried to isolate him from among all the people at the rink. He could have felt me as my eyes swept over him, the same way most everybody will feel the prickle between their shoulder blades or on the back of their neck and turn around when someone is staring at them. If the killer was a sorcerer, like Diego seemed to think—

He'd insisted on following me home to make sure I got here safely. I told him I'd already thrown up, I wasn't going to again, and I'd get home without any problem. He'd shrugged, and then followed me all the way home anyway.

33

My garage is one-car only and there's nowhere to park on the alley behind my house, so he'd parked on Hermosa Avenue, walked back over, and knocked hard on my door.

The killer had shown up twice now where I was, three times if I counted the man in the road. Maybe that was coincidence, but some protection wards had to be a good idea.

"Okay. Thanks," I said. "Come in."

He followed me down the hall to the kitchen.

"Beer?" I said.

He shook his head. I didn't know if he didn't drink at all, drank but didn't like beer, or wanted a completely clear head to set up the wards. I pulled a Corona from the fridge, popped off the top, and took a deep swallow. It felt good all the way down.

Diego had brought in a black satchel, rather like an old-fashioned doctor's bag. He hadn't had time to stop anywhere, so I assumed he kept it in his car.

"Are you smoke sensitive?" he asked, drawing from the bag a fist-sized bundle of long sage leaves tied together with a white cotton string.

"No, it's fine," I said.

My mother is a healer. I'd seen her smudge her clinic rooms at the big house with sage often enough to know that Diego was preparing to cleanse my house of any bad juju that might be hanging around me. After, he'd probably burn sweet grass to call forth peaceful energy and strength. At least, that's the way my mother always did it.

Diego drew a small silver incense burner from his bag. He lit the sage bundle with a spell, blew out the flame so the sage smoldered rather than burned, dropped it into the burner and closed the cap. He started walking around my house, striding along the inside perimeters of every room, chanting low.

I had mixed feelings about all of this. I didn't like people in my house, but Diego had been here the day he asked me to help find Brad's killer and was here now doing me a kindness. I thought briefly that the downstairs bathroom probably could use a clean before he walked into it but decided I couldn't worry about that.

I heard his steps on the stairs and felt a pang, not wanting him in my bedroom—the bed unmade, and books strewn around, not to mention the coffee cup with the dregs of this morning's brew on the bedside table—but that was a silly worry too.

He came back down, turned on the kitchen faucet and dowsed what little stub of sage was left. Then, just as I'd thought, he repeated the whole ritual with sweet grass, right down to using water to end fire.

He settled into a chair at the kitchen table like he'd been here a hundred times before. "I'll take that beer now."

I opened the fridge and pulled out a beer for him thinking it was funny that I felt safer and calmer since Diego had done his smudge-the-house-and-set-the-wards thing. I wasn't quite sure if it was the rituals or his physical presence in my kitchen that did it. Maybe I should have company more often.

"Have you eaten?" I said as I handed him the Corona and a slice of lime. The lime tree in my yard fruited most of the year and I usually kept a cut supply in a small Tupperware bowl in my refrigerator. Beer without lime was an abomination as far as I was concerned. "I could do chicken burritos."

"That would be great," he said. "Thanks."

I had half a roasted chicken in the fridge that I set about shredding. I grated cheese and lettuce, cut tomatoes, opened and drained a can of olives. All the time I worked, Diego watched me with that same relaxed, we've-done-this-a-hundred-times-before attitude he'd had since he walked in.

"When did you decide to become a wizard?" I asked just

to break up the silence. He may have been relaxed but I wasn't used to having people other than my parents around, much less to making dinner for a man I hardly knew.

He set his bottle on the table. "It was never a decision. Wizarding—is that a word?—is the family business. I'm tenth generation. I started learning the trade when I was five."

Not knowing how hungry he was, I put four tortillas in the warmer.

"What about you?" he said before I could ask more follow-up questions. "When did you first know you were psychic?"

I lined up the plates with the various burrito components along an oak sideboard that had been in my family since the 1930s.

"I can't remember ever not knowing. I guess my family is a bit like yours. Various forms of magic show up in every generation."

I took the tortillas out of the warmer and set them on a plate on the sideboard as well.

"This is make-your-own."

Diego stood, took a plate, and started building a giant burrito. I followed, building a much smaller one.

"Is everyone in your family psychic?" he asked after he'd wolfed down half of the burrito.

"Not everyone. Each generation seems to get their own gifts. My great-great-grandmother Audrey was the first one with obvious magic. She could find most anything. She was so good at finding lost people that the newspapers dubbed her 'The Bloodhound of Hermosa Beach.'" I laughed. "Not a very flattering designation."

"When was this?" he said.

"Late 1920s," I said. "Her daughter, Cassie, so the family lore goes, saved her brother from a sea goblin that had kidnapped him. She never married, but—again, family lore—they say her daughter was fathered by a selkie." I carried my plate to the table. "In my family, when a baby is born the parents gloss over the counting of fingers and toes and check for webbing in between them instead—a legacy from the selkie."

Diego used a paper towel I'd given him to wipe his mouth. "Interesting family you have."

"Um," I said.

I'd never told anyone the full history of my family. But if anyone wasn't going to laugh at it, surely it was someone who claimed to be a tenth-generation wizard.

"Go on," he said. "Who came after Cassie?"

I smiled. "Cassie and Pax—the selkie—had one daughter, Marissa. She was the first full-blown psychic, with magic inherited from both sides of the family. It was said she was also a shapeshifter. Not a selkie, she didn't become a seal, but she could turn herself into a crow to fly, a mouse to scurry away from danger, a horse to run fast. Evidently, she had to scurry away more than a few times because she had the habit of telling people what was in their minds. Some folks weren't too happy about that."

Diego smiled. "I'm guessing you learned from that lesson."

"I suppose," I said. "And experience. Once, when I was nine or ten, and already as tall as I am now, I was in the market with my mother. A tiny lady was trying to figure out how to reach something on the top shelf. Without her saying a word or even looking in the item's direction, I plucked down what she wanted and handed it to her. She was freaked out and not happy to have been given the very thing she wanted without her even asking for help. Weird, huh? I never did that again."

He laughed lightly. I had the feeling he'd had similar experiences with unappreciated magic when he was young.

"Marissa was what, your grandmother?"

I realized now there had only been girl babies born since Cassie and Pax, and all of them only children. I wondered why that was.

"Marissa married Sam Townsend," I said, "an attorney, and they had my mother, Katrina. Mom got healing ability and is a well-known heart surgeon. Dad builds low-cost housing and isn't magical at all, except for being a wonderful person. They do a lot of overseas charity work and are gone more than they're here. When they're home, they live in the same house downtown that Charles Goodlight built for Audrey in 1912."

"All of them in service to the community, one way or another," he said.

I hadn't ever thought about that either, but he was right. "Well, maybe not Marissa the shape-shifter. She seems to have blurted out whatever she read in someone's mind, helpful or not. Her habit was the catalyst for more than one divorce and at least three politicians going to jail."

"Sounds like service to the community to me," Diego said.

I laughed, but after that it seemed we'd run out of conversation. We sat at the table and ate, silence and expectation humming in the air. I felt him wondering what it would be like to kiss me and his practical mind telling him it was a bad idea and likely I wasn't interested anyway.

I wondered if he felt the same conflicting feelings from me. I'd be lying if I said I wasn't attracted to him. Something about him amused me, made me want to know more. But we'd be working together until Brad's killer was discovered and caught. Office romances were never a good idea.

Besides, I wasn't the casual one-night-stand sort and it would never work long-term between us. What I felt from Diego was he liked women, liked sex, and fervently didn't like the idea of being partnered.

Well, then, I thought, *it seems we're two of a kind in a lot of ways.*

For me, hermiting was a survival tactic as much as anything else. Being the sort of empathic psychic I was meant knowing way too much about anyone I was intimate with. Being the person I was, I didn't have much interest in being the object of expectations I couldn't escape knowing about. It was way too much pressure.

Diego glanced at his very expensive-looking watch.

"Thanks for dinner. I'll smudge your property lines and put on some extra wards on my way out."

"Thank you," I said. "I appreciate your help."

At the door there was another kiss-and-see-what-happens-or-just-leave moment.

Diego left.

5

*I*n the morning, I realized the fridge was empty of anything worth eating, unless breakfast was going to be butter, a limp stalk of celery, and a glass of almond milk. No amount of holding the door open and staring at the interior shelves was going to make food suddenly appear. Probably I shouldn't have used up nearly everything in the house making last night's dinner. I thought briefly about going out for breakfast and decided against it. Decided against going to the store, too. Takeaway it was, then.

Mickey's Deli was only a couple of blocks from my house and they had great sub sandwiches. A sub for breakfast may seem odd, but as my mother says, 'Your stomach doesn't know what time it is.'

Mid-October at the beach often meant cool mornings, warm days, and chilly nights. I stripped off the sweatshirt I'd put on first thing this morning while it was cold, revealing the navy-blue tank top I had on underneath. I slipped into a pair of flip-flops, grabbed my purse at the door—and halted.

I didn't know if the wards Diego had put on would let me go in and out of the house freely or if they needed to be taken down and put back up each time. He'd said he'd come by to pick me up at eleven and take me to the office—Fridays were evidently late starts. My '*I can drive myself, thanks*', had been ignored.

Maybe he planned to take the wards down when he came to get me and then put them back up. He'd do the same when he brought me home. I didn't like the idea of being more or less locked into my house until he showed up. I didn't really know him, but my instincts said he wasn't the type to basically imprison someone to keep them safe.

I relaxed and let my inner eyes survey the wards. They were pretty, like little sparkling lights domed over my property. They also looked like the kind I could traverse without needing a spell. I walked out the door and locked it behind me.

There weren't a lot of people on the Strand as I headed toward Second Street. I loved autumn for this—good California weather, the kids back in school, the tourists, summer surfers, and frat boys back home, and the Strand a wide-open concrete promenade mostly for locals. The ocean was a murmuring backdrop as I made my way, thinking about what kind of sub to get for breakfast.

Something about a group of young men heading toward me made the back of my neck prickle. I'm not one of those kick-ass girls who knows three types of martial arts and carries guns and knives at all times. There was a 9 mm Smith & Wesson Shield in my purse, but my preferred way of dealing with danger was to get out of the way.

I sent my psychic senses out toward the five men. Each one had spotted me, and a couple thought I was cute, but that was it. No lurking evil intentions. But the prickle at the back of my neck didn't go away.

I felt for the source and turned my gaze westward, across

41

the low concrete wall that separated the Strand from the beach. A man in his thirties, I guessed him to be, wearing a wet suit and carrying a surfboard was standing stock still, staring at me. Our eyes met. He didn't look away. Neither did I.

A sudden loud roaring filled my ears. I wobbled slightly, my knees weakening as nausea rose in me. For a brief moment I saw Brad stand beside the surfer, and then the dead man was gone—the kind of thing that you'd think you'd imagined if you didn't know better.

I knew better. I knew this was the man, Brad's killer. I stared at him hard, memorizing his features.

Except his features were changing. He'd been tallish and buff, his hair a sandy color, his skin darkened by the sun. Now he was shorter with a bit of a belly pushing at the front of his wetsuit and his hair was as black as oil. He grinned and walked toward me. I stood my ground, even when he stepped onto the Strand and was only feet away. He gave a little half-nod as he passed, as though he knew me. As though he wanted to make sure I saw him.

He wasn't here to hurt me though. Not today. I felt that clearly enough. I watched his back until he was a good twenty feet ahead of me and then followed. He turned up Fourth Place to Hermosa Avenue and stowed his board in the back of a dark blue Chevy Tahoe parked beside a meter. I took out my phone and typed the license plate number into Notes. He got in the car and drove off without so much as a glance back, but I was sure he'd known I was there. That he'd wanted me to follow him and see him drive away.

My mother is a surgeon, but she's also a community healer. I must have been about five or six when an injured shapeshifter came to our door asking her for help. She was always open to helping werewolves, werebears, and the like, and it wasn't unusual to find them at her office after-hours in either their human or animal form.

But flat-out base-shifters were not welcome, not since Audrey and Cassie's day, when a base-shifting sea goblin had kidnapped James Goodlight when he was only four. Werewolves and the like were fundamentally human, but a base-shifter was fundamentally *other*.

It was almost as if the revulsion I felt watching the base-shifter change his face and body right in front of me was encoded in my DNA. It coursed in my blood right alongside whatever it was that gave every woman in my family for generations a different brand of magical ability.

Knowing that he had murdered Brad doubled the revulsion I felt.

Doubled.

I still had that strange sense of doubling with this man— more than just the base-shifter thing. If I hadn't been so stunned at running into him practically in my front yard and then totally pissed at his 'fuck you' attitude, I would have taken a good look at him with my inner eyes.

Woulda, coulda, shoulda.

Nothing I could do about it now.

I heaved out a sigh and walked the short distance to Mickey's Deli.

The kid behind the counter was new. I was in Mickey's often enough to know everyone who worked there at least by sight, if not by name. I ordered a large sauce and cheese and pondered while I watched the kid make it. A large sauce and cheese submarine sandwich wasn't the healthiest thing— usually I got the vegetarian deluxe—but it fit my mood.

What was the doubling thing about? Why would a base-shifter kill Brad? Not that murders by shifters were any more, or less, common than murders by normal humans and probably happened for much the same reasons—anger, jealousy, and needs that weren't met.

Brad and the shifter obviously had known each other well enough to break into the rink together as a lark. How had Brad become friends with a base-shifter and why would his friend kill him? Why kill him like that—hockey stick in the belly, hockey skate blade across his throat. That was seriously personal. I hadn't known Brad well, but he didn't seem the type to get crossways with a shifter.

True, he had interned at Danyon and Peet, but if he'd met his killer through that connection, wouldn't Diego have known the shifter as well? And if Diego knew that a base-shifter and Brad were friends, wouldn't his suspicions have turned immediately in that direction?

The new kid wrapped my sandwich in white paper, put it in a bag, and held it out to me. I thanked him, paid, and walked home, still asking questions in my mind and not coming up with any answers.

D iego maneuvered his dark-blue Audi coupe through the traffic on Pacific Coast Highway so smoothly that I thought he must have been helping things along. Every time he wanted to change lanes a hole in traffic instantly appeared. We hadn't hit a red light once.

I sent my psychic senses out to feel for magic.

Oh yeah. He was using it.

I turned on my inner eyes and dug around in his thoughts enough to know that he was trying to impress me. Not trying too hard, just a little something to show what he could do. He was so nonchalant about it, if I hadn't taken a psychic peek I'd never have known. I looked away and smiled. I mean really, how often does a girl have a guy smooth out traffic just to impress her?

My good feeling faded. I had to tell him, and now seemed as good—or bad—a time as any.

"I saw Brad's killer this morning," I said.

Other than his hands tightening slightly on the wheel no one could have seen that the news affected him at all.

I plunged on with the tale. "I went out to get something to eat. I *felt* him almost as soon as I stepped out the door."

"You're sure it was him?"

"Positive. He might as well have had a flashing neon sign over his head that said murderer."

Diego grunted and slowed for a stop sign. The pedestrians on the corner motioned for him to go on through.

"So now we know what the killer looks like," he said as he accelerated. "All we have to do is put a name to the face."

"It's not that easy," I said. "He's a base-shifter. I watched him go from a tall, sandy-haired man to short with a paunch right in front of me."

His hands tightened on the wheel again, more this time.

"The good news is," I said, "I'm pretty sure I caught his signature."

"Signature?"

"Every living thing has its own signature, the frequency they vibrate to. Once I home in on it, I can follow a fresh trail pretty easily, like a hunter follows bear tracks. Older trails are harder. After a day or two, the trail is impossible to follow."

Diego glanced over at me. "I've never heard of that."

"Really?" I said, surprised.

"Can you teach me to do it?" he said. "It sounds like a good tool for someone in my line of work."

I knew the reason I could do it was my psychic ability.

45

Somehow, I assumed a wizard private investigator would have a similar skill.

"I can try. But can't you just make a spell or something to do the same thing?"

Diego shook his head. "I can see where someone is if I have something of theirs, but if they leave that place, I can't follow them. I'd have to keep casting new spells until they've stopped and stayed somewhere again."

For all that I'd paid close attention to Diego's magical driving, I hadn't paid attention to where we were going. We'd left the beach area and were headed inland.

"Where are we going?"

"Lomita," he said. "To Brad's apartment. Maybe we'll find something to connect Brad and his killer."

My stomach tensed. I wasn't at all sure I wanted to be in his apartment—to feel whatever vestiges of Brad were still there, all the while knowing he'd never return. It was too sad.

Diego flipped on the blinker and immediately traffic rearranged itself.

"His father will meet us there."

6

*D*iego put his hand out. "Mr. Keel, I'm Diego Adair. I worked with Brad at Danyon and Peet. He was a good guy."

We stood on the small, concrete walkway in front of Brad's second-floor apartment. The sorrow and confusion coming off Brad's father was so strong it made my eyes water.

When the men shook hands, I *felt* a small jolt of magic pass from one to the other and felt Brad's father let loose a bit of his pain.

"Tyron apologizes for not being here himself," Diego said. "He was called out of town. He wants you to know we're doing everything we can to find whoever did this."

Mr. Keel nodded his thanks. "You were there when they found him?"

Diego glanced toward me. "This is my colleague, Oona Goodlight. She was also at the practice that morning."

He looked me up and down. Even today there are people who don't realize women play hockey.

"You knew my son?"

I gently probed his thoughts. He hoped I'd been Brad's girlfriend—that his son had had someone special in his life. I hated to disappoint him.

"Slightly," I said. "He'd skated with my team a few times. Great guy. Good attitude. Terrific player. I'm very sorry for your loss."

Mr. Keel stared at my face. He so wanted Brad to have had a girlfriend.

He shook himself out of his unhappy thoughts, dug in his pocket, and held out a key.

"I'm having dinner with Tyron next Thursday," he said. "He can return the key then."

Diego took the key almost reverentially. It didn't take a psychic to see Mr. Keel appreciated that, that he trusted us to be respectful of Brad's things, of his memory.

I probed the man a little more, asking if he had any suspicions about who had harmed his son. He didn't. He was mystified as to why anyone would hurt Brad, which somehow made it worse for him.

Mr. Keel drew in a deep, noisy breath and held it a moment, then let it out. "I'll leave you to it then."

"Thank you," Diego said. "We won't disturb anything."

Mr. Keel nodded and walked away as if the physical weight of Brad's body weighed down his shoulders.

Diego unlocked the door and held it open for me.

I stepped into the living room and immediately stepped back. My stomach churned. My ears rang. Vertigo made the room swim as *the knowledge* hit. I grabbed hold of Diego's arm to keep myself from falling.

"Do you want to go outside for a minute?" he said. "Get some air?"

I tried to answer but the words wedged in my throat. I shook my head.

Diego slowly walked me deeper into Brad's living room and waited until my head had cleared enough for me to do my work.

It looked pretty much like I'd expect for a single guy in his twenties—decent couch, nice coffee table, huge TV screen. The one unique thing was a long shelf behind the sofa jam-packed with trophies.

I swallowed hard and found my voice. "The killer was here. He picked Brad up and they drove to the rink together."

"Makes sense," Diego said. "His car wasn't at the mall. Can you see the killer?"

I shook my head.

"You said you'd caught his signature," Diego said. "Can you follow his trail from here?"

I shook my head again. "It would lead me to the rink. They might have made a stop or something on the way, but we already know the rink is where they wound up."

"Can we go there, and have you follow it?"

I shook my head one more time. "I can't follow a trail that old."

Anger roiled around inside me—at Brad's senseless death, at it being someone he liked and trusted who'd killed him.

My voice hardened. "If I run into the killer again, I'll know it no matter how he looks. I won't let him get away a second time."

Diego lowered his chin and tilted his head.

"What?" I said.

"I didn't picture you as such a determined hunter."

"You hardly know me," I snapped. "I may be full of surprises."

"No doubt." He gazed at me steadily a moment, then shrugged. "Magic isn't always perfect either."

I gave him a wide-eyed look. "Really, wizard? I'm so disappointed."

There was no reason for me to lash out at him. I knew it was spillover anger from Brad's senseless murder and me being affected by the killer's rage, but it didn't quiet my need to strike at someone, anyone.

He looked stunned a moment, and then it was gone.

"Sorry," I said, and meant it. "Misplaced anger."

He ran his hand down the side of my arm. Just once and lightly Not so much as too seem aggressive—just enough to reestablish a connection between us, a reminder that we were on the same side and there for the same reason.

"Okay," he said. "Back to work. What else do you get from the apartment?"

I took a deep breath and let it out, to center myself, and started talking as the impressions flowed to me.

"Brad wasn't a happy soul. Felt he'd let people down. He was lonely. Felt he had acquaintances, not friends."

I saw Diego nod to that. He'd worked with Brad, but they hadn't become friends. That seemed to be the way it went for Brad.

"He did have a couple of close guy friends," I said, "and some women friends. Always friends, never girlfriends. Or if they were girlfriends, it didn't last for long. He didn't know what was wrong with him that women didn't find him worthy of love."

I stopped talking and wiped at the tears threatening behind my eyes. What a sad life—to believe others found you unworthy of love.

"But he had hockey," I said. "He was good at it. Playing silver level and had already been told he was going to be moved up to gold."

I walked over and picked up one of the many trophies. It

felt almost electric in my hands, infused with Brad's happiness and pride. He'd kept them dusted, clean.

I turned back and looked at Diego. "Why would anyone want to kill this guy?"

"You tell me," he said.

That's why I was there, wasn't it? To help catch the killer but to figure out why as well. Brad's family needed an explanation—some reason behind it, even if that reason didn't make sense to anyone but the murderer.

"I don't know why yet," I said. "When we catch the killer, he might tell us, or I might feel it. It's possible we'll never know."

I gritted my teeth. It wasn't acceptable to me that we never know why.

I put the trophy down and walked around the apartment—living room, kitchen, one bedroom, and small bath. Bed not made, dirty clothes on the floor, dishes washed though and in the drain board.

A jolt of energy, like a small electric spark, ran through me.

"Burgundy Camry," I said, as more knowledge rushed in. "A three in the license plate. Brad put his skates and stick in the trunk next to the killer's. They were laughing. Brad was a little drunk. More than a little stoned."

"Can you see the rest of the license plate?"

"No. Just the three." I pressed my lips together, thinking. "When I saw the killer, he drove a Tahoe. Why would he pick up Brad in a Camry?"

"People can have more than one car," Diego said.

"Yeah," I said, but something didn't seem right about that.

I stood a while longer listening, looking, *feeling* but I didn't get anything more.

"I think I'm done," I said.

Diego stood thinking a moment. "If you'd like, I can push a little magic into you. It might help you see more."

My stomach knotted. I've lived around magic all my life, but the idea of someone infusing me with theirs gave me the heebie-jeebies. He'd done it already with the hearing thing at the rink, and I'd watch him give a little to Brad's father, but still—

But when I thought of Brad's father, the look on his face as he opened the door to his son's apartment.

I took a deep breath. "Okay."

He stepped toward me. "Just relax. It won't hurt, I promise. You might even like it."

"Hmmm," I said, and tried hard to relax when he put his arms around me and breathed slowly in my direction.

Energy rushed through me. If I'd been on the street, I could have run a marathon.

"The killer lives in north Redondo Beach," I said, the words almost tumbling over themselves trying to get out. "A white house. There's a liquor store within walking distance."

"Would you know the house if you saw it?"

"I'm not sure. Maybe." I thought about it further. "No, I don't think so."

"Okay," he said. "That's good. We can start looking for burgundy Camrys and blue SUVs in front of white houses in north Redondo."

I stared at him. That seemed a fool's errand. There must be dozens of white houses with burgundy Camrys or dark blue SUVs parked out front or in the driveway.

My face must have said what I was thinking.

"Investigating can be very unglamorous," he said.

I gazed into his face and smiled. A new feeling was filling me. I swear I felt this weird connection to him, almost like we'd just had sex—that afterglow feeling. I wanted to snuggle against him, maybe kiss his neck.

He was still smiling. "Sorry. It's rare but it happens sometimes when I push magic into someone—it's like giving a little of myself into the other person. Most people don't notice. Brad's father didn't. You being both psychic and naturally sensitive to magic anyway, it's not too surprising it hit you strongly."

I wanted to glare at him, but all I could do was grin with that look that a former boyfriend had called 'the freshly fucked smile.' I sent my feelers into Diego's mind. He was very clearly imagining what it would be like to get me in bed.

That broke the spell.

"Dream on, wizard." I looked over my shoulder at him as I headed for the door. "Rule number one: never play where you get paid. I'll meet you at the car."

$\mathcal{D}$ iego was talking on his cell phone as he walked toward his Audi. I stood next to the passenger door. He took the key fob out of his pocket and beeped both doors open. I slid in on the passenger side, but he stayed outside, talking low on the phone. He listened, nodded, and spoke a little more, then pressed the phone off.

"We need to meet with another client in," he glanced at his watch, "fifteen minutes."

I resisted the urge to say, "Whatcha mean *we*?" I'd agreed to help find Brad's killer. I hadn't agreed to be part of a *we* meeting with random clients. Everything I'd felt in Brad's apartment was still roiling through me. I needed some time alone to sort it out.

"Can you drop me home on your way?"

Diego gave me a glance as he started the engine, his mind clearly not on me or my wants at the moment. "Wrong direction. Sorry. It's going to be tight making it on time as it is."

I tsked my tongue against the roof of my mouth, annoyed I would be stuck sitting in the car while he met with someone.

I had my phone though. As long as I had my phone, there was always something to occupy my time. I could make progress on the book I was reading. My annoyance slid away as I thought about getting back to the book I was enjoying. Double bonus—reading would help me forget about meeting Mr. Keel, and about Brad and everything I'd felt in his apartment.

We drove into El Segundo, which inevitably made me think about hockey, as there was a rink here.

"Do you ever play at Toyota Center?" I asked to make conversation since we'd pretty much said nothing to each other since leaving Brad's apartment. I'd made my feelings known about where his thoughts had wandered, but if we were going to finish this search together, we needed to be at least polite and talk to each other.

He nodded. "Wednesdays."

"Like it?"

"Sure," he said. "Great ice. Good locker rooms."

I let the conversation go fallow again. Diego obviously had things on his mind. I would have been happy for the distraction of talk, but courtesy kept me quiet.

We passed the Chevron refinery and Diego turned onto a residential street.

"I could really use your talents here," he said as he slowed the car and eased it to a stop next to the curb. "I know you only agreed to help find Brad's killer, but this woman and her daughter are convinced a witch is trying to harm them. If you'd come in and see what you pick up, I'd appreciate it."

I crossed my arms over my chest. I'd had enough of feeling other people's pain and anguish for one day. I wasn't much up for round two.

"I could give you another little shot of magic if you like," he said. "Make it easier to figure out what's really going on here."

"No, thanks."

I rolled my shoulders, trying to shake off the sad energy I'd brought with me from Brad's apartment. It worked —some.

"I'll come in and take a quick look around," I said. "Just promise that I can walk out when I want, whether you're ready to go or not."

He nodded.

"Okay, then," I said. "Just long enough to get a read and then I'm out of there."

"Thanks."

I waved his thanks off with a flick of my hand. I wasn't doing it solely for him. I'd also agreed for the woman and child's sakes. And for my own. Maybe helping this woman would help me dissolve the sad, dark fog in my brain.

Diego was good with the woman and her ten-year-old daughter. He kept his voice low and calm, never interrupted, and was patient as the woman and girl told their stories.

It didn't hurt that Diego was good-looking and projected a *complete professional* vibe in his navy suit, light blue shirt, and burgundy tie. That was a thing—attractive, well-dressed people were more instantly and generally trusted than their less attractive or more sloppily dressed counterparts. Diego made the whole package work for him

My jeans, T-shirt, and red high-tops weren't quite as inspiring, but in a weird way my look was a good contrast to his, helping the woman feel more at ease than if I'd also been wearing office formal. Yin and yang. A balance struck.

I felt around the room. My shoulders tightened. Tension vibrated everywhere I looked, but I didn't get even an inkling of magic being involved. If a witch was truly after them, there'd be magic residue, and there just wasn't any.

I sat quietly long after I'd figured out that whatever was going on with these two, it wasn't coming from a witch or any other magical source. Waited while Diego drew them out, got all of their stories, and made them feel confident that this could be sorted out and put right.

"Why do you think it's a witch?" Diego asked the mother.

"I'll show you," the woman said and stood. The daughter jumped up and grabbed hold of the back of her mother's shirt. Diego and I followed them through the house to a side door that led outside.

"These," she said, sweeping her arm to indicate markings carved into the outside of the door.

There were several standard pentacles, a square with a line down the middle and an X stretching corner to corner, a backwards capital E with a dot next to it, and three diamond shapes next to each other.

I put out my hand and touched a few of the markings. I didn't feel any magic coming from them.

Diego took out his phone and photographed the marks. He typed something—field notes I was guessing—then put the phone back in his pocket.

He stepped back and looked again at the marks for a long moment, then said, "Anything else?"

"Mama," the girl said. "The cat."

The woman drew a breath. Her shoulders shook slightly. "We both saw the cat. A huge black one with glowing green teeth and eyes. It flew at me when I was in the backyard. Scared Deena half to death." She put her hand protectively on the girl's shoulder. "And phone calls where all that's on the line is static."

Diego held his hand out to the woman. "We'll look into this. I'm confident we can end the harassment."

The woman took his hand and held it tightly between both her own. "Thank you. My daughter is afraid to be in her room at night. She follows me everywhere. We need this to stop."

"I'm going to turn this over to my boss, Tyron Danyon. He'll call you in a day or so."

"Thank you," she said again.

She still had a death grip on Diego's hand. He gently pried it loose, reached into his pocket for his silver case, and gave her a card. The woman clutched it like it was her only hope.

I stayed quiet until we were back in the car and Diego said, "So?"

I shook my head. "They certainly believe a witch is after them and I can see why with some of the things that have happened, but I didn't sense any magic at all. My guess would be that someone is trying to scare them."

"Mmm," he said. "And doing a good job of it. Any idea who?"

I felt inside myself, letting my senses roam back into the house and all around the property.

"If there's an ex with a new girlfriend, my money is on her."

"Why?"

"It's what it feels like to me. Something about the ex not really being all that ex and holding on. It's vague. I can't give you more than that."

Diego started the engine. "That's a lot, actually. It gives us a good starting point. All the client wants is for it to stop." He patted my leg in a job-well-done manner and pulled the car into the road.

"What happens for her from here?" I asked.

Diego hiked up a shoulder. "I don't see any magic in this case either. Those runes look more copied from a chart someone found online than the work of a witch. Did you see how they were both hesitant and precise? People who do magic all the time, runes are like handwriting. Once you're comfortable with making them, you get relaxed. Still precise, but relaxed. Those runes were as stiff as a child's first ABCs. No witch or wizard carved them."

I thought back to the marks. He was right about how they looked.

"But that cat thing is bothering me," I said. "I can't come up with a natural reason for a cat with glowing green teeth and eyes flying at them."

"Oh," I said as *the knowledge* made things suddenly clear in my mind. "It's definitely something with the ex. His girl-friend has a large black tomcat. My guess is florescent paint and a scared woman and child magnifying what happened in their minds."

Diego gave me an approving nod. "That's good. I'll bet you're right."

I knew I was right. That's another thing about how my abilities work. Sometimes they are spot on and immediate. Sometimes not so much. *The knowledge* comes when it feels like it. It would have been nice to have had this kind of clarity in the rink the morning we found Brad's body, to have known with absolute certainty who the killer was.

"So, now what?" I said.

"Once we turn in a report," he said, "Tyron will put some freelancers on to watch the house and see who shows up. When the agency confirms who it is, usually a simple promise to alert the police should they try it again is suffi-cient. Juliana likes to visit the perps and deliver the message. I think she gets a kick out of it."

I caught his use of the word *we* again—once *we* turn in a report—as if we were permanent work partners.

I felt his interest in me as a woman, too. Despite my never-play-where-you-get-paid rule, he intrigued me.

I tsked my tongue against the roof of my mouth. This couldn't end well.

8

The morning's events had left me hungry and since there still wasn't any decent food at my house, I had Diego drop me at the Trader Joe's on Pacific Coast Highway.

It was good to be alone. Quiet. I listened to the store's background music, bought oatmeal, bananas, bread, eggs, and a couple of prepared salads—and tried not to think about Brad or his father or that scared woman and her daughter.

I waited in line patiently, paid for my groceries, and called for a Lyft home.

The driver pulled up in front of me in a white Prius, the Lyft sign in his window, and said, "Oona Goodlight?"

I nodded, and he jumped out to help pull my bags from the cart and stow them in the trunk.

The back of my neck prickled. I sent my sense toward the driver. I didn't feel magic or evil intentions, but something was definitely off about him. With all the weirdness going on lately, I wasn't going to stick around and try to figure out what it was.

"I'm sorry," I said and gave him a weak smile. "I

completely forgot something I was supposed to pick up for my husband. I'm going to have to go back in the store for a bit." I fished in my purse, pulled a ten from my wallet and held it out.

He reached to take the money, grabbed my wrist instead and yanked me toward the open door of the back seat.

I stomped down hard on the top of his foot. He let go of my arm and I pulled it back to build momentum and punched him hard in the jaw.

Throwing a punch is like taking a shot on net—you don't aim for your target; you aim behind it. Except a hockey shot feels good. Slugging someone's jaw hurts. I shook out my hand.

The driver stumbled backwards. The curb wasn't far behind him. A hard shove in his chest and he fell over the curb, landing on his butt.

A quick glance around showed that no one else was in the parking lot—a miracle considering how busy that lot usually was—but I saw an older man and woman with their cart about to come out the sliding glass door. I reached into my purse and pulled out the Smith and Wesson, hiding it from the older couple's view behind my purse but holding it so the driver could see it.

His eyes grew big and he nodded to show he'd seen it and understood.

He levered himself up as the couple came up beside him, giving him a cursory but concerned look.

"I'm fine," he said, and laughed as though embarrassed by his clumsiness.

"Get in the backseat," I told him when the man and woman had passed.

He did. I got behind the wheel of the still-running car and hit the backseat locks before pulling the car into an empty parking slot with no other cars around it—another miracle in that lot. I turned to look at him, the Smith and Wesson once again in my right hand and pointed at him.

"So," I said. "What's this about?"

"Look, I'm sorry," he said. "Your husband, I guess it was, hired me. He's got this whole thing set up for your birthday. I was supposed to pretend like it was an abduction or something and drive you to where he's waiting. I guess the surprise is ruined now."

"Tell me about my husband," I said. "What does he look like?"

The driver shook his head. "I didn't talk to him. My agent did, I guess."

"Agent?"

"I'm an actor, but I do a lot of side gigs like this. You're not the first person I've been sent to 'kidnap.' You are the first to pull a gun on me, though."

I repositioned the gun so it wasn't pointing straight at him anymore but was still close and handy.

"Where were you supposed to take me?"

"The pier?" He said it like a question, but whoever had booked the ride needed to give a destination. And how did that person know where I was and that I would call Lyft?

I read him as telling the truth. Questioning him more wasn't going to get me anywhere. I got out of the car, grabbed a nearby empty cart, and motioned with the gun for the driver to get out.

"Put my groceries in the cart and then get out of here."

He was shaking as he loaded my purchases into the cart. When all the bags were in, I motioned with my chin for him to get in the car. He slid behind the wheel and backed out of the parking spot slowly and carefully. I watched till the car disappeared down PCH, then pulled a business card from my wallet and dialed Diego's cell phone.

———————

D iego was sitting on the sofa in the parlor and chuckling.

"It wasn't funny," I said.

He cooled the chuckle to a grin. "I know. Sorry. But he fell on his ass. The poor guy. Then you pulled a gun on him. You probably scared the crap out of him." He gave me an appraising look. "You're full of surprises, Oona Goodlight."

"Yeah, fine," I said. "But I was scared too. Someone sent him to grab me. Who? Why? How could they know where I'd be?"

A frightening thought flitted through my mind. The only person who knew I was at the market was Diego. I sought his thoughts, feeling for duplicity, for guilt, for any emotion that might indicate he wasn't who I thought he was—but there was nothing like that. Concern was in him, but only for my safety.

Diego sobered. "Good questions."

"And here's something else," I said. "I sensed magic around him, but not *from* him."

"Why do you think you felt that?"

"Only one reason I can come up with," I said. "Someone magical set the thing up."

Diego nodded slowly. "Our face-changing killer?"

A shiver ran across my shoulders. "That would be my first guess."

"Does he know where you live?"

"I'm not sure." I got up and shut the curtains on the bay

window. "Probably he does, since he knew where to be on the beach so he could show himself to me."

Diego watched me until I sat on the sofa again.

I shot him a look. "I know drawing the curtains closed won't make any difference if he already knows where I am, but it makes me feel better."

He was quiet, but I could tell the gears were turning in his brain.

Gears were turning in mine as well. I hadn't *felt* the face-changing killer who I was pretty sure was behind it, hadn't *felt* bad intentions being sent my way.

I hadn't sensed danger from the Lyft driver. Maybe because he didn't have evil intentions himself, but maybe, too, because I'd overused my abilities since finding Brad's body and was wearing them out. I'd never consider my psychic abilities finite, but what if they were?

That was a worry. It was all a worry.

Diego's gaze slid up and focused on my face. He seemed to have come to a decision over whatever he'd been considering.

"One of two things to do," he said. "One, you come stay at my place while we figure out if someone is really after you or this Lyft thing today was a bad joke or a weird coincidence. Two, I stay here."

I shook my head slightly. "Or three, I stay here by myself and take care of myself like always. Or four, I check into a hotel for a while."

He crossed his legs and leaned a little toward me. "Three isn't really an option, unless you feel like maybe being nabbed by a killer. But take your pick of one, two, or four."

"I won't be run out of my own home," I said, irrationally stubborn when I knew he had a point. But I sure wasn't going to stay at his house. He seemed nice enough, but who knew what he'd be like after the lights went out? *#Me too* was a movement for a reason.

Diego shrugged. "Then I'll stay."

My teeth clenched. I didn't want anyone cluttering up my house, taking up my time and psychological space, especially when I was still trying to sort through all that had happened this week and figure out a way to deal with it.

"You already put up wards to protect the house," I said. "Aren't they any good?"

"Plenty good," he said. "So long as you stay inside. It's Friday night. Are you going to stay indoors until Monday morning?"

The mere thought of being cooped up for two days made my stomach hurt.

I pursed my lips.

"I'll stay," he said, more firmly this time. "Your guest room looked comfortable."

I shrugged. Sometimes you have to resign yourself to the inevitable and make the best of it. Especially when deep in your heart you know it really is the smart thing to do.

"I'll put on some fresh sheets for you."

He stood. "The wards on the house are strong. No one is going to get in that you don't want in. I'm going back to my house and get a few things I need. I should be back in forty-five minutes or so."

I hadn't wanted him to stay. Now I didn't want him to go. I guessed I needed to make up my mind about all of this.

Diego did some hocus pocus at the windows and the doors—laying on extra protection, I assumed.

"You know," I said, a sudden, uncomfortable thought flitting through my mind. "The driver could have been the killer. He can change his looks the way you might change your shirt. He could show up looking like you."

"Wouldn't your psychic senses tingle or something if the killer showed up at your door?" he said.

I pushed my hair back away from my face. "They should. I seem to be a little off at the moment."

"Okay," he said. "How about a password?"

"Swordfish."

It was from an Marx Brothers movie, and the first thing that popped into my head.

Diego raised his eyebrows and laughed to himself. "Swordfish it is."

He muttered something under his breath and turned to slightly bow in each of the four directions.

"I hope you're not expecting company," he said after. "No one and nothing can cross your threshold until I get back."

I didn't know if I was grateful or annoyed at all his taking charge and protecting me stuff. Grateful, I guessed. The thing with the driver had seriously frightened me, on top of everything else that had frightened me the last couple of days.

I was annoyed, too. I was no damsel in distress. I'd dealt with the driver. I could take care of myself.

Diego pulled his car keys from his pocket. "How would you feel about learning some magic? I can teach you a few simple defensive spells that could come in handy."

"Sure." My thoughts were still churning on the Lyft driver incident and the who, what, and why. Grinding on the annoying need for protection.

"Such enthusiasm," he said.

I blew out a breath. "I get it, Diego. You're a goalie—the last and ultimate point of defense. But I'm a wing. Offense. It's my nature to drive forward, overcoming whatever and whoever tries to stop me."

He tossed his car keys from one hand to the other. "It takes offense and defense working together to win the game,

Oona. Knowing a few spells to protect yourself isn't a bad thing."

I sighed. He wasn't wrong. And he was getting my misplaced anger again.

I dropped my voice to a near whisper. "I hate being scared, Diego. Hate the need to learn spells to protect myself. Hate that Brad is dead. That a base-shifter is out there killing people and might have a thing for me. That I feel helpless."

Tears sprung to my eyes. "I hate every damn thing about this."

9

I made up the bed in the guest room and did the dishes while waiting for Diego to return. The time and activity helped me calm down and see the wisdom of learning some protection spells. Knowing more ways to defend myself didn't make me weak—it made me stronger. More competent. More capable. More independent.

And just to show that I'd put my dark mood behind me when Diego returned, I asked for the silly password before I'd open the door.

He walked in carrying a handsome dark-brown leather overnight bag with brass clasps. Either Danyon and Peet paid really well or he had another source of income. Whichever it was, he clearly liked to spend it on himself. My purchases tended toward the plain and utilitarian, but I could appreciate someone who spent the extra dollars to get nice things. It was a bonus that he had good taste. I don't think I could have tolerated a weekend houseguest who paraded strikingly bad taste.

"The guest room is upstairs," I said and led the way,

though he already knew that, having been in every room when he sage-smudged the house and first set the wards.

"Nice," he said when I opened the guest room door.

It was a nice room. My great-great-grandparents, Charles and Audrey, had only two children but it seemed pretty clear that they'd planned on more. The beach house they'd built—my house now—had three bedrooms, each large enough to have housed several boys in one and several girls in another.

Diego stood a moment taking in the ocean-blue walls, sand-colored ceiling, the king bed covered by my grandmother's handmade quilt with a large compass rose at the center. He probably hadn't paid much attention when he'd been in here before, since his mind was occupied with laying the wards. Or maybe he was just polite.

He'd been unfailingly polite, I realized. Evidently wizards raised their children to have good manners.

A family antique writing desk and chair and a wide chaise were also in the room, along with a bedside table with a good reading lamp and a bookshelf with books covering a wide swath of subjects and genres.

Some of my drawings were framed on one wall and he walked over to look at each one, spending extra time in front of an abstract of ocean. The drawings weren't signed but my hands still got sweaty and nerves jangled all over my body. I was glad he didn't ask who had done them. I was extremely shy about my art. I'd taken a few classes in college but I wasn't really trained. I drew what I *felt* as much as what I saw. Sometimes, when my psychic impressions got stuck or their meaning wasn't totally clear I'd draw to bring them to the surface. Some of those drawings were on the walls as well. I wanted Diego to like my work, but I didn't want to talk about it. That didn't make a lot of sense, but no one ever went wrong thinking humans were contradictory.

He looked up at the skylight above the bed.

"Stars at night or sun during the day," I said, glad his attention had moved on. "If you don't want one or either, there's a button on the nightstand that will draw a shade."

"Pretty cool," he said.

I shrugged. "I want my guests to be comfortable."

Diego spent his money on nice cars, upscale suits, and fancy overnight bags. I spent mine on my house.

"I've been thinking about the best way to approach the problem," he said after he'd settled his things in the guest room and come down to join me in the parlor.

I looked up from the book I'd been more leafing through than reading. "Did you come to a conclusion?"

He sat on the other end of the sofa from me. "I think I have a solution, though you may not want to do it."

The back of my neck prickled. I *knew* what he had in mind, and he was right—I wasn't sure I wanted to do it. He wasn't sure he wanted to do it either, which made the prospect more daunting.

"Have you done it before?" I said. "Pushed that much magic into someone?"

"Not quite this much magic, no. And not into someone like you—empathetic and a psychic. There might be side effects."

I could guess at the side effects. The afterglow thing, stronger than I'd felt it before. Strong enough that I'd be almost irresistibly drawn to him.

"No offense," I said. "You're good-looking enough and I like you and all, but you're not my type. So, no worries."

Which was a lie. The more I knew Diego, the more attracted to him I felt. The more attracted I felt, the more I found myself annoyed with him. Sometimes I wondered if there was something wrong with me.

"The magic will make you stronger," he said. "More capable with spells and better able to use your psychic abilities to know when danger is near. If we'd done this before I dropped you off at the market you never would have gotten near that Lyft driver. You would have known sooner that something was wrong." He paused. "You can do other things, too, with the extra magic."

He leaned forward and tucked his hands crossed at the wrists between his knees. "I see what being involved with the case is doing to you. The physical and mental pain it's causing. Let me give you the power to build a bit of a shell around yourself to help filter out the emotions bombarding you."

My eyes widened. My throat went dry. A wall to stop the assault of other people's emotions. It was like an answer to a prayer.

No, not a wall. A shell. A filter. That was fine; I'd take anything that would help me live in the world even a tiny bit more like a normal person.

"How does it work?" I said. "How does the shell get built?"

He pulled his hands from between his knees and turned them palms up. "I don't know. I know it can be done though. You'll have to figure out how to make it work yourself."

That was a lot of help. But I was smart. I could dream up a way.

"But it can be done?" I said. "You're sure?"

He nodded. "My mentor has a psychic niece. He gave her the magic and she built herself a protective net to catch random emotions and filter them out. I know it can work."

I rubbed the back of my neck, then steepled my hands in front of my mouth and exhaled a breath.

"So?" he said.

Did he even have to ask? Wasn't it obvious what my answer would be?

"Yeah," I said.

"Whenever you're ready."

"Now is fine," I said, and braced myself for what I knew I'd feel after and would have to fight down. I wanted that shell. That filter. That net.

Diego slid over next to me on the sofa, wrapped his arms around me and pulled me close so that my head rested on his chest. I heard his heart beating in a slow and steady rhythm. He tightened his hold, his hands flat against my back. He breathed into my face and I felt his magic pour into me, like being filled with liquid light. Light that drove thought from my mind. That drove out doubt and fear. Light that brought peace and surety. And power. Power like I'd never known existed. Power to do anything.

He held me a long time, long after the sense of being filled had passed and I felt his magic and power surging within me, finding its new home.

It was weird to feel so peaceful while power roiled inside me and magic crackled in the air.

"Diego," I said.

"Hmmm?"

His voice was languid. I wondered if the giver felt that afterglow connection the same way the receiver did.

If he did, if I asked him now to kiss me . . .

If I gave in to how deeply I craved feeling his lips on mine, our bodies entwined . . .

This wasn't the afterglow I'd expected. This was full-on, right-now lust.

I brought my hands up and pushed myself away from him.

"I think it worked," I said, scooting away, and coming to my feet.

His eyes were hooded. He nodded.

"This might sound crazy," I said, "but I really need to get out of the house for a while. I feel like I could run all the way to San Diego. I think I need to get out and run."

He drew in a breath and sat up straight. His eyes cleared.

"I'm not sure I'm up for a long jaunt at the moment. How about we stay here, and I teach you a spell to repel anyone who tries to grab you?"

"That could be useful," I said.

My God. The energy. The power.

The lust.

"It's a good spell and doesn't need any talismans or elixirs, just words," he said. "How good are you at memorization?"

"I took drama in high school. I was good at learning my lines."

How was I going to figure out how to build this shell/filter/net thingy? Maybe Diego would introduce me to the niece. She could tell me how she did it.

Damn, I wanted to kiss him. And more.

S unlight poured through the ceiling window. From the guest room across the hall, I heard Diego's voice but couldn't make out what he was saying. I presumed he was on the phone with someone.

The clock on my bedside table read seven a.m. I rubbed some sleep from my eyes and rolled out of bed. The morning promised one of those warm October days that made you glad to live in California. In celebration, I pulled on a pair of white denim shorts and a green T-shirt—then remembered there was a base-shifter outside, and there'd be no strolling on the sand.

I pushed my hand through my hair. No damn base-shifter was going to ruin the morning. The magic Diego had given me last night still thrummed through my body, vibrating with strength and energy, my skin barely able to contain it. He'd only given me a little push, a tiny bit of the magic in him. What did it feel like inside his skin, to be stuffed full of this power all the time?

I padded across the landing and knocked on the guest room door.

"Are you up?" I said, though I knew he was.

Diego pulled the door open. He must have woken a while ago and already showered, judging by his still slightly wet hair. He wore jeans and a blue T-shirt. His feet were bare. The scraggle along his jaw line said he'd showered but hadn't trimmed his beard back into submission yet. It was a nice look on him.

"I have something I need to do for Juliana," he said. "I can put up another no-trespass ward if you like, or you could come with. It won't take long."

"I'll come." The morning was too lovely to be stuck in the house. "Give me a minute to brush my teeth and get my shoes on. I'll meet you in the foyer."

At the door, I watch Diego take down the ward that had protected us through the night.

Once we were on the porch, Diego started to put the ward up again, but I touched his arm and said, "Can I try?"

He'd taught me the protective ward spell last night after I'd learned the repulsion spell. I'd lain in bed, unable to get to sleep for quite a while, and practiced the words. I was pretty sure I had both spells right.

"Go ahead," he said.

I coughed to cover my sudden nervousness. Why I'd asked to do this was beyond me, especially since the words had suddenly fallen completely out of my head.

So, I cheated. I pried into Diego's mind just enough to get the spell and put the ward up.

"I'd congratulate you on a good job," he said, "but I think you had a bit of help."

I shrugged an admission. "You can feel me poking around, can't you?"

He nodded. "It's like a little tickle inside my skull."

I squared my shoulders. "Take it down again and I'll put the ward up without any help from you."

He shook his head slightly. "You don't have to prove anything to me, Oona."

I felt my cheeks warm. I couldn't help myself, I poked around in his mind just a little more and smiled.

He swiped at the side of his head as if shooing away a fly.

Okay," he said. "So, now you know."

Yep, I knew. I didn't have to prove anything because he was already impressed with me.

He turned and started down the porch steps.

"Hey," I said. "I'll stay out of your mind from now on."

"I'd appreciate that," he said, turning back toward me. "People deserve their privacy."

The leather seats in his car were warm from the sun. I sank into them and listened to the music playing softly on the radio—classic rock, from our parents' and grandparents' day: "Hotel California," "Hungry Like the Wolf," "Bohemian Rhapsody."

I'd settled in, tapping my foot in time to the beat, thinking it was a nice day for a drive, when the back of my neck prickled, and my hands began to itch.

"Stop the car," I said.

Diego kept his eyes on the road. "Why?"

My chest felt tight. "Just stop the car. Now."

His lips pulled in a taut line, but a hole immediately opened in the traffic and he guided the car into the parking lot at the Manhattan Beach mall.

I didn't wait until the Audi was completely stopped before I jumped out.

Diego was out and beside me in seconds.

"What's going on?" he said.

I flitted my gaze left and right. "He's here. Somewhere nearby." I pulled my gaze to him. "Remember I told you I had the killer's signature and I'd know it if I felt it again? He's here."

I caught it again, like a scent on the breeze, and stalked off toward the stores to follow it.

Diego caught my arm. "Don't be crazy. If he is nearby, you can't just go chasing after him."

I pulled my arm free of his hold. "We can. The two of us."

He didn't look happy. "How close is he?"

I cast my senses out, feeling for the killer, but I'd lost the signature.

"He's gone now." I slumped a little, disappointed in myself. "He was probably in a car and drove on by. I shouldn't have had you pull over."

"Do you know for sure he was in a car?"

I shook my head. "He was close and now he's not. That's the best reason for that to happen that I can come up with."

"You're sure he's not around here now?"

"No. Definitely gone."

"Then let's get back in the car and finish what we started to do."

Diego opened the passenger-side door and held it for me, then walked around and slid in behind the wheel.

"The killer was nearby," I said firmly.

He started the engine. "I believe you."

I sat in silence a bit, feeling stupid and berating myself. I was tempted to peek into Diego's thoughts and see if he really did believe me but resisted. He was right—people deserved their privacy. I was going to have to take him at his word.

"Where are we headed?" I said, making my voice light in the hope that my mood would follow its lead.

"To see a friend who has some information for Juliana."

I cleared my throat. "But where are we going?"

Diego pulled onto the freeway and did that thing again that made traffic open up for us.

"Disneyland," he said.

"Mickey has some info?"

"Not into the park, actually," he said. "But close by. One of the parking lots."

"Ah," I said. "The lot attendant?"

Diego shot me a quick, exasperated look.

"I should stop asking questions?" I said.

"Let it be a surprise," he said and leaned forward to change the channel on the radio.

I resisted the urge to comment on his new choice of music —headbanger metal—and sat back trying not to think about sensing the killer's signature and losing it like that. I didn't know what I could have done differently. I'd felt the signature, knew it was close, but didn't have any sense whether the killer was in a car or walking, or what direction he was moving. If I couldn't figure out a way to home in on it more, I might as well not feel the signature at all.

Diego pulled off the freeway and we followed the signs to parking for the Disneyland Hotel. We passed a number of open parking spots as he drove to the very back of the lot and parked next to a strip of well-manicured greenery. He glanced at his watch and got out.

I wasn't sure if I should go with him or stay in the car, so I sat.

"You coming?" he said.

I slid out of my seat and joined him as he walked toward the greenery. Something moved among the well-tended flowers so perfect they almost didn't look real—tall red tulips in bloom out of season—a flash of gray among the green stems and leaves.

A large opossum stepped out onto the asphalt. The air shimmered and a very good-looking man who I guessed to be maybe twenty stood where the possum had been.

Diego and the man embraced and exchanged a bit of greeting. I stood there, my mouth a little agape, but neither of them seemed to notice. Diego didn't introduce us.

The man reached behind into a back pocket of his jeans and pulled out a large manila envelope that was much too big to have fit there. He handed the envelope to Diego.

"Thanks," he said.

The other man nodded, the air shimmered again, and the man was gone.

I waited until we were back on the freeway and headed north again before I said, "What was all that?"

"Kingston?" Diego said. "He's a fairy and a shifter. A lot of fairy-men are shifters but for some reason instead of being wolf, bear, or whatever big beastie, they seem to choose smaller animals for their alternate form."

"Okay," was all I could say. I'd known human shifters and though I'd never met a fairy before I didn't discount their existence. If there were fairies, it wasn't a far stretch to believe there were fairy-shifters just as there were human ones. And if the fairy wanted to be an opossum, who was I to judge?

As to how an opossum carried around that large envelope or how the fairy fit it into the small back pocket of his jeans —I guessed that would stay a mystery to be solved another day.

"Did he give you what you needed?" I said.

"It's for Juliana," he said. "I have no idea what's in the envelope."

"Because she's the boss?"

"Because everyone at Danyon and Peet minds their own business unless asked to be involved."

I nodded, taking that in. Every company, like every team, has its own culture. I was still figuring out how things were at Danyon and Peet. Being a private person myself, knowing that no one there would get all up in my business made me happy.

Diego, I guessed, was the exception to the don't-stick-your-nose-where-it's-not-wanted rule, given that he'd jumped all over making sure I wasn't alone and unguarded. Not that I'd minded all that much, so far. I could see, though, that the 'woman in jeopardy/knight protector' thing could get old really fast.

"*W*here does Juliana live?" I asked as we drove north on the 405 freeway.

"Holmby Hills. Mapleton Drive," he said, and let it lay there.

I would have whistled, but that seemed a little rude. Mapleton Drive didn't even have homes that sold for less than nine million dollars, and those were probably teardowns. The Spelling mansion, known as The Manor, was on that street—once, and maybe still, the most expensive estate in the country.

"She doesn't believe in your magic," I said.

I was pretty sure Diego already knew that, but it had struck—and bothered—me when I'd met her.

He grinned. "She doesn't believe but she does, if you know what I mean. Her rational, surface mind says magic doesn't exist, but deep down she knows all about me, and now about you. She knows that things happen in the unseen world and that sometimes they spill over into the ordinary world and wind up at the door of Danyon and Peet, but she'd rather pretend everything had a rational explanation."

I knew exactly what he meant. I'd experienced the same sort of thing with friends and non-magical family. One part of them dismissed magic or psychic ability out of hand. Another part couldn't deny things they'd witnessed that couldn't be explained away. It must be confusing for them and easier to develop a sort of convenient blindness than contemplate what real magic in the world might mean. We humans had amazing capacities to believe what we wanted even when all the facts said otherwise.

"What would you tell Juliana if she asked where you got whatever is in the envelope?"

"The truth," he said. "I always tell her the truth. She chooses to believe instead that I'm brilliant and resourceful." He flipped on the car's blinker. "She's half right."

"Which half?"

The traffic opened up and we pulled off the freeway at Sunset Boulevard. "I am exceedingly resourceful."

I chuckled under my breath.

"What about Mr. Danyon? Does he believe you're a wizard?"

"Tyron is, uh, more willing to suspend disbelief."

"Does he believe you about my psychic abilities?"

Diego nodded. "Psychic abilities seem not only possible but plausible to both Tyron and Juliana. Much more than pure magic. It's funny, because we take cases that involve the supernatural or people in the magic community; we're known for it. Juliana and Tyron manage to convince themselves there's nothing unusual going on when clients come in with problems that turn out to be a ghost, or poltergeists, theft by gnomes—whatever."

We wended our way east, up into the hills. Most houses in the area were behind high privacy-inducing hedges and tall, old growth trees. All the greenery and the hidden houses made the neighborhood almost country-like. The ultra-wealthy liked their surroundings pretty. I was more than happy to enjoy it too.

Juliana's house, more an estate really, was set far back from the road. Only a small corner was visible when we stopped, and Diego punched in the code to make the black iron gates part so we could drive in.

"Who else lives here?" I said as the giant home came into better view. The two-story house was done in a French Château style, white with gray trim, with small balconies in front of the upstairs bedroom windows, and a tall chimney at either end. The grounds were as well kept and tastefully done as the house, with yew hedges and a row of tall, thin Cypress lining the circular driveway.

"She has a cook and housekeeper who live in," Diego said.

"No family?"

"She says she's too busy for a family or even a love life," he said. "She thinks she's fooling people. She's been off and on with a musician who lives in Venice for as long as I've known her. He's fairly famous. I think she tells herself she's keeping the relationship secret for his sake, but the truth is that Juliana likes to project this aura of married-to-the-job-and-you-should-be-too." He shook his head. "Stupid way to live."

He stopped the car in front of a set of tall double doors painted a deep dark red.

"Do you want to go in and see the place? Otherwise I'll just drop the envelope and we'll go."

Curiosity urged me to join him at the door to at least get a peek inside. I would have liked a full house tour, I loved seeing how people lived, but didn't think I much wanted to put up with Juliana's attitudes at the moment.

"I'll wait in the car."

Diego took the manila envelope he'd gotten from the fairy/possum, trotted up to the door and knocked. The woman who answered the door wasn't Juliana. I thought she was probably the housekeeper. Diego handed her the envelope and headed back toward the car, pulling his cell from his pocket, and answering a call as he walked.

He stopped, bent his head, and listened hard to whatever was being said. He nodded and pressed the call off.

"That was Tyron on the phone," Diego said as he slid behind the wheel and closed the driver-side door. "This sounds a bit like a game of telephone: a friend of Brad's called Mr. Keel, who called Tyron, who called me. This friend of Brad's wants to talk to us."

"Us?" I said.

"According to Tyron, yes—both of us."

A shiver of nerves shot through me. My head began to ache. I had one of those sudden and clear realizations I get from time to time. *The knowledge*—information that came unbidden that I had no logical way to know. Over the years, I'd learned to trust the knowledge when it showed up.

"The friend is the killer," I said softly, sure of it. "Drive fast. He's desperate."

"If this guy is the killer," Diego said, "you can't go waltzing up to him, not if he has some sort of thing for you."

He had a point, but the desperation I felt wasn't aimed at me. It was turned inward.

I shook my head. "I'll be all right. If it feels dangerous to either of us when we get there, we'll turn around, okay? But right now, we need to hurry."

Diego's mouth drew into a tight line, but he nodded.

W hen we reached the address Tyron had given Diego, I felt around for the killer's signature but didn't find it. Diego must have not sensed any danger either, because he pulled the car to the curb and shut off the engine. A tall, rangy man about my age with a mop of brown hair stood in the driveway of a small, white, 1950s tract house. An older burgundy Camry was parked on the street in front. There was a three in the license plate.

"I'm Eric," he said as he led us to an even smaller back house that still left room on the lot for front and back yards. "Thank you for coming."

"No problem," Diego said. "I'm Diego." He glanced my way. "This is Oona."

"I know who you are," Eric said as he opened the front door. His vibe was a mixture of tension and relief.

I *felt* again for any danger to Diego, or me, but there wasn't any. As to how he knew who we were, I supposed Mr. Keel had given him our names.

But who was he? The *knowledge* said Eric had drawn his skate blade across Brad's throat, but he didn't feel like the killer. That didn't make sense, but I couldn't shake the feeling.

We followed Eric inside to a sparsely but nicely decorated living room. The gray-tweed couch facing the television looked new. I figured the slightly scratched bentwood rocker was a family hand-me-down.

"I don't have much to offer you," Eric said when we were settled on the couch. "You wanna Coke? Or some water?"

Diego and I both shook our heads.

Now that we were in the house, Eric's distress poured off him in waves. I felt his guilt and remorse deep in my stomach. Diego and I waited him out in silence, letting him pick the time to speak and the words to use.

Eric sat on the edge of the bentwood rocker, popped the tab on a can of Coca-Cola and took a deep drink. I watched his throat work as he swallowed. He set the can on the floor by his feet.

"I know you know," he said, his eyes locked on us.

Diego nodded slightly, a motion that seemed to indicate we knew a lot more than we actually did.

The torrent of emotions that flew from Eric threatened to give me a migraine. I clasped my hands tightly together in my lap. A long silence stretched out between us.

"I didn't do it," Eric said suddenly. "I mean, I did do it, but it wasn't me."

Diego leaned forward, his hands between his knees, and waited for him to go on.

Eric's gaze darted around the room before settling on us again.

"It was like being possessed," he said, his voice a thick whisper. "My hands on the hockey stick, my feet inside the skates, but it wasn't me who killed him. It wasn't *me*. Does that make sense?"

Diego nodded slightly again.

My stomach was twisting itself into knots from the remorse coursing through Eric. All the extra magic Diego had poured into me last night had heightened my normal sensitivity without providing any sort of filter. The threatened migraine hammered in full force. Spots danced in front of my eyes.

"He was my friend," Eric said. His eyes filled with tears. "Why would I kill him?"

Diego reached a hand toward the distraught man. "You need to call the police. You need to tell them what happened."

Eric swallowed hard. "I know. I just wanted to tell you guys first. Because you knew Brad. Mr. Keel told me you found him, and you knew him, and you were looking for the killer. I lied to Mr. Keel. Told him I had some information about Brad's death and I'd only tell it to you." He laughed without humor. "I guess it wasn't such a lie."

His voice broke on the last word. I wished Diego would pump a little magic into Eric to ease his pain, but he didn't seem inclined to.

Eric sniffed and cleared his throat. "Anyway, yeah. I wanted to tell you first. Sort of practice before I call the cops. Mr. Danyon said I could trust you."

"You can," Diego said. "We won't turn you in if you don't want to go to the police. But you should. They'll find you eventually. It's better if you go to them."

Eric picked up the Coke can and squeezed it between his hands. "You want to know something bad? Even while I was hating myself for what I was doing, I was enjoying it too. That's the part I can't stand. That I liked doing it."

His words hit me like a physical blow. I put my hands over my heart, for protection.

I knew Diego saw my motion from the corner of his eye, but he kept his focus on Eric. He reached into his pocket and pulled out his phone.

"How about I call the cops for you," he said. "We'll stay until they get here."

Eric nodded in a bobblehead sort of way and stood.

"I gotta take a leak," he said and headed for what I assumed was the bathroom.

The door shut with a solid click.

Everything in the room turned suddenly red. Red walls. Red furniture. Red air.

"Diego," I said, pushing his back to get him moving. "Go after Eric. Hurry."

Diego was halfway there when the shot tore the air.

Evening had long since turned to night by the time we started the final leg back to my house. We'd been hours with the police, and a small time with Brad's father and Tyron at Mr. Keel's hillside house in Palos Verdes.

Not that having a name for his son's killer and knowing that person was now dead soothed the loss for Mr. Keel. In a perfect world, our children outlive us. It seems the natural order of things. In the real world, fate can be a complete bitch. We left Mr. Keel staring out the big plate glass slider that offered an ocean view below and a sky view above. It was a beautiful night, the air clear, the sky star-filled. I don't think Mr. Keel noticed.

The hum of the engine and the wheels turning on the road were the only sounds as we came down the hill, the lights of the flatlands twinkling below. A sight that usually cheered me. Tonight, it made me sad.

Sorrow followed us into my house. Deaths like Brad's, like Eric's—stupid, senseless death—could only bring sorrow to everyone it touched. Eric had a family just like Brad did. A pair of cops would be showing up at Eric's parents' door with the news that their son was dead. Would they tell the parents they also suspected their son had murdered his friend or would they save that for later—a double whammy of grief?

"You want a beer?" I asked Diego once we were back in my house and I'd turned on every light downstairs.

He sat on the sofa in the parlor and shook his head. "I don't know. Maybe."

I sat beside him, the sides of our thighs barely touching. I hadn't known him long, but this was the first time he seemed not in complete control of the situation and himself. I laced my fingers together lightly and rested my hands in my lap.

He smiled thinly, put his arm around my shoulders and pulled me to him. There was nothing romantic about it—just two profoundly shaken and sad people finding comfort with the other.

"Eric was so unhappy," I said. "He could face admitting what he'd done, could face prison, but he couldn't face himself."

"Because part of him enjoyed it."

I nodded, my head against Diego's chest. "The one pain he couldn't bear."

I sat up. "Or maybe not part of him. In my vision, there was this weird doubling sense I had of the killer. What if Eric was right when he said he'd felt possessed? That it wasn't him who killed Brad. Eric wasn't a base-shifter. Is it possible that someone or something else had taken him over?"

"Sure," Diego said. "It's possible. A malevolent spirit could do it. Some of the creatures in the Brume can take over another entity. Either could be a base-shifter. That's what you feel happened?"

"Yeah," I said. "I don't know who, what, or how. My sense is that Eric is gone, but the killer isn't."

I opened my third eye and let words spill out as sensations and knowledge rippled through me.

"I feel the killer," I said, "but I can't describe him. No, not him. *It*. Something alien, something you might run into on another planet or in the dark deep of the ocean. It's not like anything I'm familiar with to make a comparison. *Alien*. That's all I can tell you."

Diego nodded. "Probably something from the Brume then."

I cocked my head.

"The Brume," he said again. "The place of murk and fog."

"What do you mean?"

"There's our world," he said, his hand sketching a vague circle in the air, "and there's the place where the happy dead go." His other hand sketched another small circle in the air. "The Abyss is where the unhappy dead reside—ghosts, ghouls, vampires, and the like. There's Wonderland, home to fairies, garden sprites, elves, brownies, all the good beings that fill our fairytales."

He stopped and regarded me. "You've never felt these parallel worlds?"

I hiked up one shoulder. "I seem to be grounded in our world. Tell me about the Brume?"

His face clouded. "It's where monsters are born and live. Some are made by black arts wizards and witches. Some come into being spontaneously. Everything there is filled with anger and hatred. It's a very unpleasant place."

A tremble ran across my shoulders. "So, one of these creatures could get into our world and take someone over?"

"It's rare, but it can happen," he said. "The walls between worlds aren't walls at all—more like membranes that thicken and thin over time. Black magic practitioners sometimes thin the membrane more, to bring across whatever they've called. Sometimes other things slip through."

"That's what you think this thing is, something evil that slipped through?"

He nodded. "Because you said it felt alien. The beasts and beings of the Brume are so completely different from us or anything in our world that alien is the only word for them."

Diego steepled his fingers in front of his lower face and let out a long breath.

I bit my bottom lip. "This is something bad, isn't it? Something really bad."

He stood. "I'm going to check the wards again. Then we should both get some sleep. Tomorrow we'll go see a friend of mine who's an expert on shadow beasts. Maybe he can help."

S ome nights a boatload of brilliant stars shine above the ceiling window in my bedroom. Tonight, a wet, gray fog filled the night sky.

I'd punched up a YouTube video on my phone of mediation music, the drone-y kind that seemed to work best for me when I had trouble sleeping. There were mandala visuals, but I'd shut my eyes against them and focused on my breathing: deep breaths in, complete breaths out. Reaching for that relaxed state and those slow theta brain waves that can bring creativity. Because I needed all the creativity I could muster to dream up a way to build a defense against other people's emotions.

We humans are silly creatures sometimes, but here's the thing about being an empathic psychic: even when you don't rummage around in someone's mind, you can't help but be aware of feelings. Not just the strong ones—love, hate, jealousy, rage, desire—but even the little things. Even when the emotions didn't shout, they were there, tiny pinpricks wanting attention, small wants, small disappointments. It was exhausting—and the reason I hadn't had a boyfriend in three years and only one or two close friends at all. It was better to be alone. Easier.

I wanted to drown out those persistent voices. I wanted it to be easy to be with people. A way to let me live in the world almost like a normal person.

Ironic that the tool for giving me that normalcy was magic.

I felt the new magic in me slow as my breathing slowed, flowing through my body like a lazy river. It felt a natural part of me now, as if it had always been there. Magic that had been a gift given with no expectation of anything in return. I'd find a way to thank him though. Something would present itself. Life seemed to work that way.

Deep breath in. Complete breath out.

It was useless. Thoughts zipped and zinged inside my skull. Brad. Eric. The killer. The Brume. Diego.

And my immediate, personal problem: how was I going to turn raw magic into a shield for my psyche?

I pressed my phone open, shut off the meditation music, and stared into the dark.

In the morning I whipped up scrambled eggs with mushrooms and onions, added cream cheese for richness, and made cinnamon toast while Diego walked the perimeter of my property making sure the wards were strong.

I'd thought about him a lot through the long night and watched him now as he ate. It was better to think about him than Eric and Brad. Much better than thinking about a base-shifter killer or the Brume. Diego Adair was beginning to grow on me.

Or maybe I was just lonely in the face of all this death.

"Who are we going to see today?" I said. "Some friend of yours who knows about shadow beasts?"

He nodded, his mouth full. He swallowed and wiped a napkin across his lips.

"Maurice," he said. "He's an expert on metals and on the creatures of the Brume. If there's anyone who might know what possessed Eric, it's Maurice."

"I'll drive," I said, because my life had fallen into crazy-land with murders, suicides, and things from the Brume. I needed to feel capable and in control of something at least.

We went out to the garage and I slid behind the wheel of my little yellow Subaru. I pressed the button on the garage door opener and backed into the alley behind my house.

"Where to?" I said.

"Just up Pier Avenue."

I took Fourth to Hermosa Avenue and then to Pier and made a right. Traffic was always bad on Pier Avenue where it ran through our cramped downtown. There are several four-way stops on the road and always a line of people in cars waiting their turn to go. Traffic was one of the few downsides of living at the beach and the reason I walked whenever I could.

We were almost to Pacific Coast Highway when Diego said, "Turn in here behind the Civic Center. Go down and all the way to the back of the lot."

I followed his directions and pulled into a spot at the back. I thought Maurice must work in one of the buildings, but Diego got out and walked to a little patch of weedy greenery near the vacant tennis courts. What was it with Diego's friends hanging out in the shrubbery? I slid out from behind the wheel and stood near him.

A huge gray rat trotted out from the plants and headed straight for us. I jumped and gave a small yelp.

Diego grinned. "Did I forget to mention Maurice was a rat?"

The rat stood on its hind legs and bowed.

"Nice to meet you," the rat said, and then laughed. I'd never heard a rat laugh but the high-pitched sound couldn't have been anything but laughter.

Maurice didn't feel like Diego's fairy-shifter friend who wasn't the animal he'd first appeared to be. Maurice felt like a rat.

"Nice to meet you," I said, trying to sound as if I spoke to talking animals every day.

Diego sank down and sat cross-legged on the asphalt. I shrugged and followed his lead.

"Did you bring me something?" Maurice asked.

Diego pulled a bit of napkin from his pocket, unfolded it, and offered its contents to the rat.

"Cinnamon toast!" Maurice said. He picked up the bit of bread with his front paws and set to nibbling.

"It's polite to bring a gift of sweets when coming to Maurice for help," Diego said to me.

The rat stopped eating. "Damn right. This is pretty good, too. You make it?"

Diego tilted his head in my direction, giving credit where credit was due.

"Good toast, lady," the rat said.

"Oona is a psychic," Diego said. "She has a sense about a creature that might be around town, something from the Brume. I hoped she could describe it and you might know what it is."

Maurice stopped nibbling. If a rat could look suddenly somber, Maurice did. He set down the crumb of toast and focused on me.

"When did you first notice the creature?" he asked.

I told him the story of finding Brad dead and the sense of doubling I'd had in my vision of the murder. I talked about Eric, how he said he'd felt possessed. I told the rat how Eric was dead, but I was certain the killer was still around. I told him how I perceived the killer.

"Alien and formless isn't much to go on." Maurice said when I'd finished. "Besides, I don't know of any creature without a shape. Everything's got a figure of some sort. Even base-shifters have a basic form."

"Not formless really," I said. "I'm sure it has a shape; I just don't know what it is yet."

The rat picked up the toast again and nibbled. He stopped and looked at me. "What you're describing is almost certainly from the Brume, but I need more to go on to give it a definite name."

Diego pulled to his feet. "We'll work on that. Thanks for your time."

"You're welcome," the rat said. "Always good to see you. Bring a whole piece of toast next time. I have a family to feed, you know."

We got back in the car and pulled out of the lot. I made a right off Pier to Pacific Coast Highway.

"About Maurice," I said. "He's not a shifter like your possum-fairy friend, is he?"

"No," Diego said. "Maurice is just a rat. A magical rat, but a rat."

I shook my head slowly. "There's a whole world out there I never knew about."

"Worlds," Diego said. "Worlds next to worlds. Worlds intersecting and overlapping with each other. "

"Not what we see on the surface," I said.

"Nothing like what we see on the surface."

"Yeah," I said. "Part of me knew that—my family history and all."

"Only part of you?"

I shrugged. "My parents tried to give me a normal life, an ordinary life. I think partly it was my dad not being magical himself, and partly my mom's pushback against her own childhood with a shape-shifter mother who pretty much blurted out every psychic impression she ever got from someone. My mom hides the source of her abilities in the normal world. I only knew how magical her healings were because she had wizards, shifters, and others as patients up at the house. The wizards and witches would do magic that I'd see sometimes, so I knew magic was real, but that world wasn't my world, if that makes sense."

The back of my neck prickled, and I jerked my head to look out the driver-side window.

Diego touched my arm. "What's wrong?"

My hands were squeezing the steering wheel. My jaw had clenched so tight it hurt.

"I've caught his signature again. I'm going to follow it."

From the corner of my eye I saw Diego's hands tighten to fists.

Traffic was as slow on this stretch of the Pacific Coast Highway as it was in our small downtown—two narrow lanes going each way, with an equal amount of space allotted for parking as for driving. I cursed under my breath as the car in front of me slowed, stopped, and then started to back up to parallel park alongside the concrete median. I glanced at Diego. It would have been good if he'd done his traffic trick, but maybe that only worked if he was driving.

After what seemed an excruciating wait, we moved forward again, crossing Herondo Street and into Redondo Beach. My shoulders pulled up near my ears of their own accord. The signature was stronger now, the trail fresh. The killer, I thought, had come down Herondo and turned left.

Every block we went brought us closer to our quarry. My pulse thudded at my temples. A tension headache formed a crescent of pain along the right side of my head.

At Pearl Street, I turned left. The signature was stronger now, so strong I not only felt it but seemed to hear, see, and taste it—a low buzzing in my ears, a dark shimmer in the air, the taste of dirty metal in my mouth.

I turned left again at Camino Real and felt a blow to my chest. A blow that came from nowhere and nothing. I grunted low.

"You okay?" Diego said.

My hands were so tight on the wheel that my knuckles had gone white. I nodded that I was okay—as okay as I could be. The buzzing in my ears grew louder.

"Damn," Diego said.

A block up, the police had erected a barricade. Half a dozen black-and-white police cars, the light bars on top flashing red and blue, and an ambulance were beyond it. Cops swarmed around an old beach bungalow painted a faded green. Wood sawhorses with yellow tape strung between them closed off the street from through traffic. I pulled the car to the curb and parked.

My throat felt tight. I centered myself and opened my inner eyes.

A shudder ran through me. I reached out into the mind of the cop who looked to be in charge.

"It's happened again," I said. "The cops have the killer. He hung around after, dazed. It's the victim's best friend since grammar school."

"Like Brad and Eric," Diego said.

"The real killer is gone now." I shook my head, sorting

out the various feelings running through me. "It brought us here on purpose—to show off its handiwork. It wanted us to know."

Anger bubbled through me. "We have to stop this thing. We have to find it, corral it, destroy it. Whatever it takes."

*E*xhaustion hit me then—an irresistible force dragging my eyes closed. I could barely force them back open.

I slowly forced my head around to face Diego. "Would you mind driving us back?"

The fatigue and sorrow in my voice must have been as clear to him as it was to me.

"Sure," he said, concern clear in his voice. "No problem."

We got out and exchanged places. I leaned my head against the glass on the shotgun side and closed my eyes. I guess I dozed off, because it seemed that the next second we were parked in my garage.

Diego slid out on his side and walked around. He opened the passenger door and helped me out.

"A wizard and a gentleman," I muttered, taking his offered hand.

"Self-preservation," he said. "You don't look like you'd make it into the house without falling. All I need is a cranky invalid on my hands."

I started to smile, but the sudden change in Diego's expression stopped me.

"What?" I said.

He slipped his arm over my shoulders and pulled me close.

"Tell me," I said.

"Someone tried to breach the house wards," he said, keeping his voice low.

The back of my neck prickled, and my shoulders tensed.

"The killer," I said, my voice as quiet as his had been.

Diego nodded, confirming what I already knew. I felt the killer's signature swirling in the air like a fog of gnats or dirt in a dust storm.

Why had he felt it immediately, but I hadn't until I sought it out?

I wondered again if I was using up my abilities, that I'd wake one morning and find them gone. There was no one I could ask, no one I knew who was psychic like me, no one who'd run her abilities far more than normal who could tell me if I could lose them from overuse. Diego had said use would strengthen them like a muscle. It didn't seem to be working that way.

"Let's walk around front and past my house," I said, wide-awake now. "I need to see if the signature fades or if it's still nearby."

"Not a good idea if the beast is still hanging around."

I moved my shoulders in the barest of shrugs. "I can't think of another way to be sure."

We walked five houses down. The signature lessened, fading like acrid smoke cleared by a sea wind.

"It's gone now."

I turned and fished in my purse for my keys as we walked back to my place.

Diego took down the wards, I unlocked the door and we went inside. As soon as the door closed behind us, Diego shot the wards up again.

"It's after you," he said.

"It could just as easily be after you," I said. "You've been staying here. Maybe it doesn't like having a wizard on its trail."

"More likely it doesn't fancy having a psychic who's caught its signature coming after it."

"Maybe it doesn't like either of us very much," I said, trying to make light of the situation while my heart thudded. It was my house the beast had tried to breach. But both Diego and I were here. Was the killer after one of us or both?

"Is there any way to know when it tried to breach the wards?"

Diego shook his head. "Why?"

"What if," I said, thinking it through as I was speaking, "the beast came around, tried to get in but couldn't. It somehow knew where we were, the route we'd likely take home, and intentionally left its signature to draw us to the murder in Redondo Beach?"

"It's possible," Diego said. "Especially if it wanted us to know what it had done there."

"A brag or a warning? The beast saying: look at me—I can lead you anywhere I want, and I know where you live. Or: even if the wizard's wards stop me at the door now, eventually you will be just as dead as this man."

Both possibilities gave me the shivers.

"It won't get past my wards," he said. "You can count on that."

I grabbed Diego's arm. "Maybe: I can make one of you do this to the other."

He put his hand over mine where I clutched at him.

"That's not going to happen, Oona. But the quicker we figure out what beast we're dealing with and how to stop it, the better."

Easy to say, 'That's not going to happen.' If Diego attacked me physically or with magic, there'd be little I could do to stop him.

"I might be able to draw a picture of the killer," I said.

Diego's eyebrows rose. "I thought you didn't know what it looked like."

"Sometimes when I get a vague psychic impression, my subconscious knows more than I think it does. I draw to let deep down knowledge percolate to the surface."

"It's worth a try," he said.

Diego followed me into the third upstairs bedroom, the one I used as studio space when I felt creative. I took a large drawing pad out of the closet where I kept my supplies and sharpened a number two pencil. Usually I drew with colored pencils, but now plain gray lead seemed right.

I pointed to an overstuffed chair and ottoman in the corner. "You can sit there." I hated having people looking over my shoulder when I drew.

I sat on the tall barstool at my drawing table, closed my eyes, and let my hands tell me what my conscious mind couldn't. When I felt done, I opened my eyes and looked at what I'd drawn.

"Come see," I said.

I'd drawn an animal, but it was no animal I'd seen in life. Four-legged, gray, and standing on its hind legs, it looked like a cross between a warthog with sharp horns protruding from either side of its mouth and a toad with its dry, leathery skin covered with bumps. Diego looked at the drawing and winced.

"Do you know what it is?" I said.

"I'm pretty sure, but we should take this drawing to Maurice in the morning and see what he has to say."

"Can't we go now?"

I didn't want to wait another day to find out what this thing was and if there was a way it could be stopped.

Diego shook his head. "Maurice always knocks off work at noon on Sundays, for family and pack time. Not to mention that one of his wives is about to drop a new litter. Even if he were at home, he wouldn't talk to us now."

I blinked, taking that in. Magical rats. Magical rats with scheduled family time and multiple wives.

I drummed my fingers against my thighs. Waiting until tomorrow made me want to scream.

Diego took hold of my hand, flipped it over and put two fingers on my wrist, as if taking my pulse.

"Hmmm," he said in a very badly mashed-up accent. "Ze patient 'as 'ad ein rough week. Fool of ze shock. Dr. Adair prescribes rest and relaxation."

I shook my head. "How can—"

"Shhhh, fraulein," he said and lifted my wrist to his ear, as if listening.

I laughed once, lightly.

Diego lowered my arm and turned it loose. "Ja. Rest and relaxation. Perhaps a game? Ze patient plays ze games? Boggle? Monopoly?"

"I'm not really much for board games or house games in general," I said. "I don't have anything here."

"No," he said in his normal tone. "What's this then?"

He turned his back to me and bent his head toward his chest. I heard him murmuring the sorts of words I'd come to recognize as spell sounds. He turned around and handed me a beige cloth bag closed by a blue drawstring.

I pulled open the drawstrings and laughed. "Jacks? You carry jacks around with you?"

He sent his gaze toward the ceiling and then back at me. "That would be pretty silly. No, I conjured them."

I looked at the bag in my hand again. He'd done exactly what he'd set out to do—distracted me from my dark thoughts. I appreciated the effort.

"Conjured? Really?"

He opened his palm and showed me three small quartz-looking stones in his hand. "Watch."

He closed his palm, murmured some more words, and was somehow holding a long-stemmed red rose. He handed me the flower.

"How do you do that?" I said over my shoulder, heading down the hallway to the kitchen to get a vase for the rose. He didn't answer until I came back to the parlor and set the vase and single rose on one of the end tables by the sofa.

"Tell me how you do that," I said again. "How you make things appear out of the air?"

He shrugged and grinned. "Well, I'm a wizard, so there's that."

I half-rolled my eyes. There was something to be said for a man who knew how to change the subject when things looked dark.

"Can you teach me?"

"If you promise to, I don't know, watch a movie and chill for the evening or something. You really need some R&R. I do too."

I frowned, wondering if I *could* relax. "I promise."

"Good," he said. "To conjure, you have to see in your mind's eye the thing you want to bring to you. It has to be something real. You can't summon up a unicorn. Do you have something in mind?"

I nodded.

"You'll need these," he said, handing me the three small rocks. "You need something real for the spell to attach to. It doesn't have to be these particular stones, or stones at all, but it helps if whatever you use has been infused with power."

I looked at the tiny rocks in my hand and then at him.

"Repeat the words I say," he said. "I'll go slow."

Again, I didn't see the actual moment the object came to me or came into being—however it worked—but as soon as I finished the last word, I had a small replica of the Stanley Cup in my hands.

I held it out to Diego. "For you."

He smiled. "Sweet choice. Hold it a moment." He drew in a breath, closed his eyes a second, and then drew in the air with his finger. "Okay, turn the base and take a look."

I chuckled. He'd inscribed both our names in with the names of all the NHL players who'd ever won the cup.

He reached for the replica. "I'll treasure this always. Or until the illusion fades. Whichever comes first."

"Illusion?" I said.

"Sadly, yes. When you get up tomorrow, the rose and the cup will have faded away." He half-shrugged, probably in reaction to the disappointed look on my face. "Magic can do many things but bringing real objects into existence isn't one of them."

That made sense. But if the things conjured were illusions—

"Then why can you only conjure things that exist in the real world? Why can't you conjure a unicorn?"

His brow furrowed. "I don't know. I was told early on, when I first learned the trick when I was a kid, that only real things could be conjured. I took my dad's word for it."

"So, you never tried?"

"No," he said.

I raised an eyebrow. "Shall we try?"

He thought about it. I felt his curiosity and his hesitancy.

He shook his head. "Maybe another time. Now, pick a movie to watch. Something light and funny. Though, maybe not a chick flick."

Here was another of those times when I wanted to peek into his mind. Why the hesitancy? Was there a reason for not conjuring an illusion of an illusion that he, for whatever reason, didn't feel like telling me? Was it dangerous? Did he not want to think that his father had told him something that wasn't true? Was he just tired of magic tricks and not in the mood? I could have asked, but I was tired too.

"*Cool Runnings*?" I said, naming an old movie about the first Jamaican Olympic bobsled team.

"Perfect."

We settled in together on the sofa and I turned on the movie. I'd seen it maybe half a dozen times, and evidently, he had too, since he talked along with some of the dialog. When he put his arm over my shoulders, I nestled into his side. My mother says, 'Physical human contact is powerful medicine.' She's right.

He'd been right about watching a movie. It was a good distraction, a way to not think about all that had been happening. When the final credits rolled Diego said, "I'm bushed. Bedtime for me."

He kissed the top of my head lightly, turned, and went up the stairs as casually as if we'd been friends and roommates for years. I waited fifteen minutes, feeling the heat of that soft kiss radiate through me, then went up to my bedroom.

Alone in my room, I heard him in the shower, singing an old Van Morrison song, "Into the Mystic." Like me, he must have been raised on his parents' old music. He sang with enthusiasm and completely off-key.

T he sky seen through my ceiling window was clear, the stars a spill of diamonds on black velvet. The dim squeak of my bedroom door sent adrenaline shooting through my body. I *felt* him standing in the doorway, his presence as strong as if trumpets had announced his arrival.

Just because we'd cuddled some during the movie didn't give him the right to come into my bedroom at midnight expecting—who knew what? I turned my head toward him.

My voice was ice. "What are you doing here, Diego?"

"Nothing sinister," he said. "And not what you think."

"Oh?"

In the faint light I saw him appraising me. I felt his annoyance, and his fatigue. "You and I both know we'll be together eventually."

"Really?" I said. "You're pretty sure of yourself."

"About this, yeah. It's inevitable. You already wait, holding your breath, wondering, wanting, and not wanting. Right now, you're hoping first one thing and then another."

I didn't say anything.

"Look, Oona," he said, "The last few days have sucked. Brad. Eric. The guy in Redondo. Beasts from the Brume. Only a fool thinks mixing sex up with fear and sorrow is an okay idea."

My voice stayed cold. "And yet, here you are."

He ran his hands through his hair. "You don't make things easy, do you? Men get sad, too, you know. Men get lonesome. Our hearts can ache. All I want is a warm body to curl next to and a good night's sleep. That's all I came for. It's all I ask."

That was all I felt from him, too—the simple desire for companionship. The healing power of human contact.

I'd sold him short, not given him credit for being just as human as anyone else, for having the same natural emotions. It was pretty crappy of me.

But what did I want? The question had a simple answer: the same thing he'd asked for.

I twisted, lifting myself up on one elbow. "You sing off-key."

He tilted his head in acknowledgement. "So I've been told."

"Stay," I said.

*I*n the morning, I put on the electric kettle as soon as I heard Diego coming down the stairs.

"Breakfast tea with zoom-loads of caffeine?" I said when he padded barefoot into the kitchen, his longish hair uncombed. "Or something calmer—chamomile maybe?"

"Tea?" he said, sitting at the oak table. "Nothing more substantial?"

The kettle clicked off and I poured boiling water over a bag of Morning Thunder for me. "Maybe later. Right now, all I can think about is taking the drawing to Maurice, getting this bastard demon-beast named, and figuring out how to stop it."

He ran his hands through his unruly hair. "I'll take caffeinated, thanks."

I put a fresh bag of Morning Thunder in a mug, poured hot water over it, and passed him the mug. My new supply of magic thrummed in my blood, urging me onward. I wanted him to hurry and drink his tea so we could get moving.

"I've been thinking," he said. "It might be better if you

stayed home and I brought Maurice to you. You're safe here, behind the wards."

I blinked, annoyed. "Don't get all overly protective on me just because you spent the night in my bed."

Diego lifted his arms in a stretch. "Quiet mutual comfort is hardly the same as having passionately fucked our brains out. Even then, I'm hardly likely to suddenly become Mr. Chivalry. I am concerned for your safety though."

I stared at him, stunned. "I can't believe you said that."

"Just being honest," he said. "Do you not like your friends to be honest with you?"

"I'll tell you what, Dee—"

His eyebrows shot up. "D?"

I shrugged. "I woke up this morning and the name in my head for you was Dee. Just the front half, not the whole Diego. Too many syllables."

He rolled his eyes. "Preferable to the back half, I guess."

I scoffed. "Eggo? Yeah, much better than that."

"We're getting off topic," he said.

"On purpose," I said. "To spare you making useless arguments."

I dropped my voice back into friendlier tones. "It's true I hide out at my house a lot, but I have my reasons and it's by my choice. It was my choice to agree to help you find Brad's killer. I'm not going to stay here while you hunt this whatever and bring it to heel. It'd be better if you taught me more magic to protect myself."

He closed his eyes a moment and sighed. "It would be best if you didn't go running headlong into trouble. And fucking great if I didn't have to worry about fighting off some demon-beast from the Brume out on the street."

I saw his point—sort of. I saw, too, that he didn't know me.

I stirred honey into my tea. "It's my nature to fight my way to the goal."

He muttered something I didn't quite catch. I didn't need to hear the words. His body language and vibe were loud enough.

"This isn't a game," he said. "The demon-beasts in the Brume have no conscience, the way we understand it. No regard for others. No remorse over killing."

That sobered me.

"Thanks," I said quietly. "It's a good reminder, but I'm not going to stay home. I'm going wherever this hunt takes us." I licked my lips. "You put up a good front, Diego, but the truth is you want me beside you in this fight."

He stared at me a moment and then laughed softly under his breath. "Never work with a psychic."

"Too late," I said. "Now you're stuck."

He turned his hands palms up. "I talked Juliana and Tyron into hiring you, so I guess I hung myself."

Diego had led me to believe the first day he came to my house that Tyron wanted to hire me. My first day in the office, Juliana had called me Diego's new hire. I guessed I knew which it was now.

"Why did you do that? Your bosses seem to give you a lot of free rein, but not enough to hire someone purely on your say-so."

"You'd had a vision of the murder. I thought you'd be able to help find the killer quickly; bring Mr. Keel some kind of closure. His wife died two years ago. Cancer. Then he lost his son, their only child. I figured, why not bring you on board and see if you could help bring him some peace."

The weight of that responsibility settled hard on my shoulders. What if we failed? What if we never could bring any peace to Mr. Keel? What if we couldn't stop the killer from hurting more people?

There was only one answer: we wouldn't fail.

Diego drained his mug and set it down. "We'll take the drawing and your car and go see Maurice," he said. "Do you have anything sweet around? Cookies?"

I remembered he'd said that an offering was expected in return for Maurice's expertise.

"I have some chocolates."

"That's perfect," he said.

I took several of the dark chocolates with caramel filling out of the plain brown box and dropped them into a plastic sandwich bag. I was glad Dee had abandoned the idea of me staying home under some sort of protective house arrest. But I couldn't shake the feeling that I hadn't won as much as I thought. That he'd walked me right where he wanted me to be and I'd hardly noticed.

The same parking spot at the back of the lot behind the Civic Center was open and I took it. It was Monday but except for two other cars the lot was empty. Maybe the people who worked here disliked driving in town as much as I did. Whatever the reason for the mostly empty lot, picking the same spot seemed right somehow.

I turned off the engine, picked up my drawing, and Dee and I exited our respective doors. Maurice already sat on the asphalt just outside the green strip he evidently called home.

"What did you bring me?" the rat asked, his pink nose twitching.

I thought for a moment he meant the rolled up drawing I carried, but realized he meant the treat.

I sat down on the asphalt next to him and took the chocolates out of the bag.

"A friend of mine makes these," I said. "I only share them with those I consider special and worthy." Still a little miffed at Dee, I leaned close and whispered, "I didn't offer any to Diego."

Maurice chuckled his rat laugh, then eagerly took a small nibble from the candy I'd set in front of him. A shiver of pleasure shimmied the length of his body.

"This is delicious," he said. "My compliments to your friend."

"I'll tell him," I said, and imagined the conversation: *Good news, Jeff. Maurice the rat thinks your chocolates are grand.*

We waited while Maurice nibbled away half of a chocolate, then heaved his little shoulders and sighed. He sat up and gave a shrill whistle. Three rats ran from the greenery and eagerly hauled the rest of the chocolates back with them.

"Okay," Maurice said. "Let's see what you brought to show me."

Dee had remained standing. He sank down on his haunches next to Maurice. "Oona did a drawing of what we think is probably the thing that killed Brad."

I unrolled the drawing and spread it out flat for him to see.

Maurice blinked. "Bring me a brick or something. I need to get up higher to see it properly."

I went back to the car and grabbed my large, carpetbag-like purse. I carry a huge purse since I like to be able to drop anything I might buy or pick up into it—regular women's pants being decidedly skimpy on pockets. I brought it over and set it on the ground for Maurice. The rat scampered up, stood on his hind legs and looked down at the drawing."

114

"You're pretty good," he said to me.

"Thanks," I said. "Do you know what it is?"

"Sure," he said, and looked at Dee. "You know what it is, too."

He nodded. "But I wanted to be sure."

The rat nodded, too. "A Klimertin. From the Brume. A nasty piece of work."

"Tell us what you know about it," Dee said.

"The klim," Maurice said, turning his back to the drawing to face us, "feeds on emotions, especially fear. The Brume is full of emotion, creatures full of rage, of hate, and their own desperate hungers. I'm surprised this klim would leave a place of plenty—from its point of view—and venture out here, where it seems to have found a need to manufacture the strong emotions it hungers for."

"I think it might be stalking Oona," Diego said. "Any guesses on why?"

The rat sat back and considered me, his nose twitching. I felt him poking around inside my mind a bit—odd to feel in myself what I've done so often to others. Dee was right; it feels like a tickle on the inside of your skull—but I felt the rat reaching out more to the klim, poking around inside it. Searching. Searching.

"Got it," Maurice said. "The klim is focused on Oona because she's full of conflicted emotions, which the klim finds a delicacy. She hides away from the world for self-preservation and yet hates the need, which she views as a weakness. She loves and doesn't love her psychic abilities."

He shifted his gaze to Dee. "But what the klim really likes is her conflicted feelings for you, Diego." The rat turned his gaze back to me. "It would be better for everyone if you'd make up your mind." His whiskers twitched, and he heaved a small rat sigh.

I felt my cheeks warm and glanced at Dee, but his face was calm, as if he were interested in what Maurice was saying but it had nothing to do with him. I wanted to take a look at Dee with my inner eyes, see how neutral he really was, but held off. I'd promised him privacy and meant to keep my word.

The rat looked up at the sky, as if finding more answers in the clouds, then back at us. "Both of you are providing plenty of lust—honestly you two reek of it—which the klim likes, but it can find lust anywhere. What the klim smacks its lips over is Ooona's conflicted and confused state. The klim loves those 'don't know what the hell you want' emotions roiling around inside. Umm. Yummy.

"Diego here is more forthcoming. Some good old lust and some growing affection. Boring—as far as the klim is concerned. But you—" he pointed a paw at me, "all that desperate need for privacy to protect yourself from the onslaught of the world, that 'don't want to need anyone, don't even want to want anyone' stuff, but seriously wanting to jump Diego's bones and have your way with him, and maybe love him a little—the klim eats that up."

He paused a moment. "The klim is after you, Missy, because it's more than a little worried you might find and hurt it, and because you feed it so deliciously. Conflict is its bread and butter."

The rat reached a paw behind his ear and scratched. "For gods' sake, Lady. Just bang the boy. You'll both feel better and the klim won't find you quite so alluring."

My cheeks flamed. I stared at the ground. I was hardly the only emotionally conflicted person in the world. I wasn't even the only person putting off a would-be lover that she maybe didn't want to put off forever but wasn't ready for now. So why me?

"Did someone or something bring the klim here, or did it slip into our world on its own?" Dee asked.

The rat shrugged his shoulders. "Ask the psychic. Isn't that why you brought her on in the first place?" Then he laughed, that high-pitched rat laugh.

"I can't read you, Maurice," I said. "I don't know if it's your ratness or your magic that keeps me out, but when I try to know your thoughts, I get nothing. I can't read the klim either. I can feel its presence, follow its trail, but I can't catch thoughts or feeling from it. I certainly can't read if someone brought it or it came on its own."

I thought about the implications. "We need to know that answer, don't we? Need to know if we're chasing only the klim or chasing the klim and whoever engineered its move into our world."

Maurice turned his gaze to Diego. "She's pretty smart. Do you listen to her? You should."

Dee gave the rat a closed-mouth smile. "She's plenty smart. I pay attention."

"Good," Maurice said. "The next step is up to you, wizard. Use that big magic you're so famous for and find the answer to that question."

Maurice sniffed and trotted on back into the shrubbery. Evidently, he'd said all he had to say.

Dee stood and reached out his hand to help me up.

"Look," he said when I was standing, "I'd already figured out most of what Maurice said about you. Well, except the part about you wanting to move to the next level. You did a good job making me think we were firmly in the friend zone and that wasn't going to change."

I eased my hand free from his. "Maurice may be a magic rat, but that doesn't make him right in everything he says."

Dee gave me a close-mouthed smile. "He's right about that, though. But I won't rush you."

I sent him side-eye. "My high school boyfriend was the first and last man to rush me into anything."

"I believe that."

He shook his head and I felt memories sliding through him. "The teen years aren't easy on anyone."

He had that right. "At least they're behind us now."

"Yeah," he said. "Thank God for that."

As we eased out of the parking lot and back onto Pier Avenue I said, "Are you really famous for your magic?"

"No," he said. "Known, maybe. In small circles."

Pride has a distinct color, a rather nice purplish blue. I watched his aura flare with the shade.

False modesty is pretty stupid when I can see how you really feel, I wanted to say.

This was exactly why I didn't want to be involved with any man, much less a full-of-himself wizard who evidently was as perceptive—about some things at least—as he was magical. My whole life was a case of too much information.

And yet, there was something about Diego Adair. Something that, if I didn't explore the possibilities, could leave me wondering *What if?*

Not to mention that the klim was out there inciting people to kill their friends, and oh, by the way, stalking me because my internal conflicts tasted most delicious.

*D*ee had been quiet on the short drive back to my house, but his busy mind had pricked at me—bits of thought poking into my awareness—like listening to someone mumble under their breath, catching a word here and there, enough to know the general direction of his thoughts but not the particulars.

We pulled into the garage, stopped the car, and went in the back door.

"Would it help to say what you're thinking out loud?" I said, taking a seat at the kitchen table. "You feel pretty jumbled. What's going on in your wizard brain?"

Dee sat and fiddled with his empty mug from this morning, still on the table. "How would you feel about staying at my place for a while?"

"Why?"

"The klim is a nasty beast. The wards here," he glanced around to indicate my house, "are strong, but my place is pretty much a fortress."

You can't be the sort of person who voluntarily puts

himself in front of a bunch of big strong guys shooting heavy pucks at your face and body at fifty miles an hour and up and doubt your ability to stop whatever someone throws at you. If Dee thought I'd be safer at his house, who was I to argue?

"For how long?" I said, realizing I trusted him now, when I hadn't before. Maybe it was feeling the truth of his promise not to rush me. Funny what a difference a few days can make.

He shrugged. "Until the klim is back where it belongs and you're out of danger."

A day? A week? A month?

"Okay," I said. "You pack up your stuff and I'll pack up mine."

I have something of a fetish about checking out people's homes. The best way to know someone is to read their mind. The second-best way is to see how they choose to live.

Dee's home wasn't what I expected. He'd said he lived alone, and the two-story, red-tile roofed Spanish-style houses that stretched nearly property line to property line with just a bit of land around its perimeter struck me as too large for one person. The teensy bits of land around the house were carefully planted and manicured. I'd bet good money it was kept perfect by a paid gardening team—or by magic.

It was a wizard's house though. The front door lacked a doorknob, keypad, or any other way to open it that I could see. I smiled, a little proud of myself for noticing that just before he muttered a spell and the door swung open. As we stepped inside, I saw that the door was covered in runes, visible now but not when we'd stood in front of it.

He led me to the living room and motioned toward a

light-colored linen sofa. I settled myself on it, surprised how comfortable it was for having very modern, sharp lines.

"Can I get you anything?" he said. "I have cold water, orange juice, and I think there's some beer."

"Water would be lovely," I said.

The rest of the room's furniture was new and eclectic—a big flat-screen TV mounted on the opposite wall from the couch above a low Japanese wooden chest with a frosted glass front that held components.

There were a couple of comfortable-looking casual chairs and one of those lift-top coffee tables that converted a sort of TV tray for eating. Two oak Empire-style chairs for when extra seating was needed, I assumed, stood against a wall.

Dee was a chameleon on the street, equally believable in jeans and work boots, a perfectly tailored suit, or anything in between. His home, though, definitely said he was a single man who liked his peace and his creature comforts.

He brought me a glass of water. I took a sip and held the glass.

"You're practically vibrating," I said, thinking maybe he was more like me than I'd thought and was uncomfortable with people in his house. "What's on your mind?"

"I need to mix up a potion," he said. "And we need to talk."

"Okay," I said.

Curiosity pricked at me, but if he'd wanted to tell me more, he would have. I'd promised not to poke around in his head. So far, I'd been good about keeping that promise, but life might be easier—for me at least—if I broke it.

He waved vaguely in the direction of the carpeted stairs. "I keep the magic stuff up there. My tools and whatnot."

I started to stand, but Dee shook his head.

"That room is private," he said. "No one's ever been in it but me."

"Oh. Okay," I said and sat back down. The desire for privacy was something I could appreciate and respect. I pulled my phone from my purse and punched up the book I'd been reading.

He stood a moment, then motioned with his head toward the stairs. "The hell with it. Come on."

"Are you sure?" I said. "I'm fine here. Really."

He shrugged. "Why not? We're in this together."

I tucked my phone back in my purse and followed him up to the second floor. I felt honored by the invitation.

At the landing at the top of the stairs, I looked around. The house was vaguely L-shaped. There was one door in the middle of the bottom of the L and two doors along the long side. All the doors were closed. I followed behind as he strode toward the first door in the long side of the L, muttering as he approached. The door swung open and he went into the room.

I stood in the doorway and took in his wizard's lair. The walls were painted a bright white. A long farmhouse-style wooden table sat beneath a large window with a view over his backyard. The one chair in the room was pushed up to the table.

Rows of bottles holding various wet and dry ingredients, several silver, copper, and glass bowls, and boxes of differing sizes holding who-knew-what waited on shelves and table-tops. An extensive library of leather-bound books, some with arcane writing on the spines, filled a bookshelf that took up most of one wall. Everything was as neat and orderly as the landscaping outside.

"Shit," Dee muttered. "Chair."

I squeezed up against the jambs as he rushed by, out into

the long hall, and disappeared into the room on the short end of the L. He returned with a tan canvas director's chair that he set in front of the wall opposite his workbench.

"Thanks," I said and sat.

He stood looking at me a moment as if wondering if inviting me in had really been a good idea, then turned and walked over to his workbench.

I cleared my throat. "Is it okay for me to talk? Can I ask questions, or do you want things quiet while you work?"

He'd settled into the chair at the table and twisted to look at me over his shoulder. "Talk is okay. Questions are okay. But not too much of either."

I could appreciate a desire for not too many words. I did have an immediate thought though.

"The question we're looking to answer is if the klim came into our world on its own or someone or something brought it."

"Right," he said.

"How will you find out?"

Dee drew in a breath and let it out. "I can't. I don't know any magic that will answer the question. Maurice was right. It's something you have to discover psychically."

I shifted my gaze around the room, as if an explanation might hang in the air. No answers floated by. I looked back at him.

"Then why are we here? I thought it was up to you and your magic to find the answer."

He nodded. "It is, at first. Then it's up to you. I can make a potion and cast a spell to temporarily enhance your abilities. Sort of like what I did for you at the rink, enhancing your hearing, but it's a lot easier to up one of the five senses than the sixth. That takes extra, specific magic."

A thrill of nerves ran through me.

"You can say no," Dee said. "If you don't want to do it, we'll either find another way or go without that question being answered."

"You've already pushed your magic into me a couple of times," I said. "You mean giving me even more? A bigger dose?"

He shook his head. "That magic is in you now, more or less permanently. I'm suggesting an elixir to give you a temporary boost."

"More or less permanently?"

He cleared his throat. "Some of that magic will find a happy home within you and stay. Some will fade. You'll always be more powerful than you were before, but in time, you'll be less powerful than you are now."

"Okay," I said, wondering exactly how all of this worked.

A thought struck me. "When you give me some of your magic, does that mean you have less?"

"Temporarily," he said. "It comes back though. The tank tops itself up pretty quickly."

"Okay," I said again. "Good."

I took another swallow of water and held the glass between both hands. "Tell me about this elixir."

Diego hiked up a shoulder. "Like I said, it will enhance your sixth sense. Hopefully, it will help you find out if the klim brought itself over or had help."

I nodded. "If the klim brought itself, all we have to do is stop it."

I couldn't believe I'd said 'all we have to do' as if bringing down the klim or at least sending it back to the place it had come from was some easy task.

"But if someone brought it," I said, "that person could probably bring more things from the Brume. These deaths could go on and on. Deaths that could be only the beginning."

Dee inclined his head, agreeing with me.

"I'll do it," I said.

"Good," he said. "Come over here and I'll walk you through what I'm mixing."

I stood next to him while he poured out a bit of this and some of that, naming each ingredient, pulverized a bit of amethyst and some azurite and added that in, then mixed it with filtered water. I wasn't quite sure about drinking rocks but decided to trust that Dee wouldn't poison me.

He strained the mixture through cheesecloth into a silver glass, then handed me the finished product.

I held the glass for a moment, uncertainty rushing through me again.

"What, exactly, will happen once I drink this?"

"Your third eye will open wider than you thought it could. You'll be able to home in on the klim wherever it is—in the Brume, in our world, or some other—and read it. Hopefully, you'll find out how it got here and what it's after."

"If the potion opens my third eye, will I physically go to the Brume or will what I see be a psychic vision?"

"I wouldn't ask you to go into the Brume alone. It will be a vision, but it will seem real." He dropped his voice so low I barely heard him add, "If this works."

"It'll work. I have faith in your magic."

Dee blushed. That was a first.

I still hesitated, nervous over how the potion would affect me, especially since he'd pushed all that magic into me the other night. But if I believed my own words, everything would be fine, and we'd discover a truth we needed to know.

I lifted the glass to my lips and drank the whole thing down.

Nothing happened.

"You might want to sit down," he said.

I walked back to the chair he'd brought for me and sat.

"I don't feel any …"

My ears popped, the same way they had at the ice rink. Dancing sparks of every color filled the room. Every inch of my skin tingled. The taste of coffee with milk, of all things, filled my mouth. My chest seemed to expand, and I inhaled great breaths of air filled with the smell of old leather, the individual fragrances of every plant, stone, earth, feather, and wood in the room—and Dee's scent.

God. Dee's scent. Like the air after a rain, dark cocoa, and cloves. Each scent distinct, following one on the other. I felt drunk on it.

But I couldn't linger breathing it in. My third eye warmed and the world opened to me. I felt tied to every leaf, every bird and beast, every human. To the hills and valleys, to the sea, sky, and stars.

Then worlds opened. Ours, and the fairies', and others I couldn't name. And the Brume. My head pounded, and bile rose in my throat.

The Brume. Dark and busy with shadow-things flitting here and there. Things without form, only black emotions. Things with forms, twisted and distorted. Things shaped like humans but without faces.

A land filled with anger. Hunger. Misery. Rage. Danger.

I walked in that dark land, my heart pounding, searching for the klim's trail.

Hands reached for me from the darkness. Claws of unseen beasts racked at my skin. A wall sprung up to my left, black brick and impossibly high. In front of me stretched a long featureless desert, yellow sand glinting strangely in the darkness. To my right ran a wide river of bubbling red liquid. Trapped between them, all I could do was keep moving forward.

Something creaked to my left. The wall. Creaking, creaking. Cracking. Black stones fell, crashing into the yellow sand, falling from the apex like an avalanche. I ducked down, my arms over my head, and ran. A brick the size of a large man's fist hit my shoulder. Pain shot down my arm. I kept running.

Thunder rolled in the distance. The dry ground turned marshy and sucked at my feet. Fear twisted my stomach.

Anger. Anger. Rage rushed through me. I could have burned the land with a thought.

"Fuck you, fear," I yelled, anger fueling me. "You don't know who you're dealing with."

The stones stopped falling.

Low growls filled the air. My eyes darted left, right, forward, up, down behind—searching for the source of the growls.

A beast, striped yellow and black, like a tiger, but huge, with red eyes and long gleaming fangs sped toward me out of the darkness. Its speed terrified me. I maybe had a minute. Maybe less, and it would be on me.

The stones began falling again. The tiger spread leathery yellow and black wings that had been folded tight against its body, huge wings, camouflage-striped the same as its fur. It took to the air.

Tricks or treats. Bricks or beast? Which would get me first?

Dee was with me then. I couldn't see him, but I felt him, heard him. Dee muttering his spells. Dee shaking some sort of gourd, its dried seeds rattling louder than the crash of falling stones, louder than the tiger-dragon's roar.

But he wasn't here. It was only me the tiger-dragon would devour.

Dee still chanting, his words echoing inside my mind. Power surging through me. Protection coating my skin.

I picked up a broken, baseball-sized piece of brick. I'm tallish and I'm strong. I understand about mechanics, about not facing the target, but standing sideways, about not opening up my hips. I cocked my right arm all the way back and heaved it toward the tiger-dragon. The thing screamed as the stone smashed into its left eye. I grabbed another chunk and threw it, hitting the beast in the soft underside of its throat. The thing screeched and wheeled away, flying off across the endless desert.

I ran again. Ran until the wall beside me had completely crumbled, revealing the membrane behind it. The membrane was thick and gelatinous when I pushed at it. Like pushing my fingers into a bowl of dirty lemon Jell-O.

On the other side of the membrane, things moved. Human shaped things. Dog-shaped. Bird-shaped. Cow-shaped. Our world.

I trotted over the marshy soil with my head in the air now, searching for the klim's signature. And found it.

The trace was faint, but unmistakable. I stopped and let my third eye lock on to the klim, find its trail and follow it.

The trail led along the membrane separating our world from the world of the shadows. Here and there I came on places where I could *see* the Klim had thrown itself against the divider. The further along I went, the more frequent and powerful the thrusts had been.

And then, a ragged hole—the door the klim had used to come into our world.

The next moment I was back in Dee's house. He had a firm hold on my left hand. Tension had tightened his face. Eyes closed, he muttered spells that sounded like the desperate prayers of the damned.

I blinked, orienting myself back to this world.

The spell casting stopped. Dee opened his eyes.

"Oona?" he said.

"Yeah," I said. "Back."

Back and myself again, except for the anger pulsing through me.

"You said it wouldn't be real," I snapped. "Maybe it wasn't, but it seemed very real. I was terrified. Don't ever ask me to do anything like that again."

"I won't," he said, letting my hand loose. "I promise."

Moments passed. Neither of us spoke. Dee kept his gaze on my face, searching for something. The answers, of course. The worry in his eyes didn't change.

Slowly, slowly, my anger drained away. We had to know the answers I'd gone looking for. I'd agreed to take the potion. Nothing was his fault.

"Sorry for being a brat," I said.

He smiled thinly but said nothing.

I shook myself out of the last of my rage. It wasn't really my anger at all. It belonged to the Brume and should have stayed there.

But the thing I had learned there, and the fear it had shot through me—that stayed. I forced my voice to be calm.

"I found trace of the klim. I followed the trace to a hole in the membrane between its world and ours. It came over on its own. The Brume is filled with emotion, all of it dark, but it didn't satisfy the klim to feed on that. It was starving. It's here to ease its hunger."

Dee nodded, but still didn't speak. At least his face relaxed some.

I fell silent, too. I wanted to tell him the other thing I'd learned, the thing I couldn't stop thinking about. But what was the point? He'd only worry. Only steal away the last of my independence in the guise of protection.

I could use his protection. Needed it. What sort of fool was I to count independence and solitude as more important than safety?

"There's something else," I said. "The klim wants me dead."

15

*D*ee's face clouded. "Maurice said the klim was feasting on your indecision. Why would it want you dead?"

I tried to speak, but my thoughts still weren't ordered. I tried again.

"Do you remember I told you about my great-grandfather, Pax, who was a selkie? And Cassie who destroyed a sea goblin?"

Dee nodded.

"In the Brume, I could read the klim's thoughts. It's old. Old enough to have known both of my great-grandparents. The *gremhahn*, the sea goblin, wasn't the only base-shifter they'd gone after. The klim used to be an ocean creature. Cassie and Pax forced it into the Brume. Somehow it figured out who I am. It wants its revenge on Cassie and Pax for driving it out of the ocean to the dry land of the Brume. Killing me is that revenge."

Dee looked deep into my face. "That won't happen, Oona. I won't let any harm come to you."

I desperately wanted to believe his words. "I felt you helping me there in the Brume. The strength. The protection."

"Just protection," he said. "The strength was already in you. You pulled that out of yourself, not me." He gave me a level gaze with a hint of a smile. "I told you before you were totally badass, probably the most badass woman I've ever known. I may have to marry you."

He meant it to lighten the mood, but I couldn't shake the fear and dread the klim had set in me. It wanted to kill me. And not quickly, either.

He sobered. "It takes a lot of guts to venture into the Brume and keep going the way you did, even in a vision."

My throat tightened, and tears flooded my eyes. I choked back a sob.

Dee poured another glass of plain water and held it out.

"Drink this. It'll help get the elixir out of you. And the tension. Get you grounded back in our world."

I took the glass but didn't drink. There was something I needed a lot more than water. I needed Dee's strength, the feel of his skin, and the warmth of his arms. The comfort of human contact.

"Would you mind hugging me for a while?" I said.

Dee smiled in that closed mouth way he had and said, "I wouldn't mind. Let's go downstairs."

He took my hand and led me back to the living room. We settled on the couch. I felt a little silly now for the request, but Dee put his arms around me and held me close like we'd sat this way a thousand times. I wondered again if he felt the afterglow the same way I did, if him pushing his magic into me was equally intimate for both of us. I leaned against his chest, sinking into him, hearing his heartbeat. Needing the comfort. The safety.

The enhanced senses I'd had in the Brume had faded, but

I still caught Dee's scent—clean air after rain, dark cocoa, cloves. I'd been this physically close to him before I'd drunk his potion. He'd smelled good then, but not like this. Now his scent was both a lullaby and a siren song. I liked it. A lot. Maybe too much.

Afterglow.

My eyelids grew too heavy to hold open. I let them close, breathed in his scent, and slept.

I woke with a start, my heart pounding, and bolted up into a sit. The room was dark, unfamiliar. Dee lay on his side on top of the covers I was under, facing me. His eyes were closed, his breath soft and rhythmic. I stared into the darkness, my mind full of the awful realization that had woken me.

"What is it?" he said.

For a moment, I thought he knew I'd had an insight and was asking specifically about that. Then I realized his question was general—was I thirsty? Did I need the toilet? Was I trying to puzzle out how I'd gotten to his bedroom when I'd fallen asleep on the couch?

"Dee," I said, my voice low, not wanting to shatter the peace of the night, though there was no way not to now. "The klim brought itself over. No help from anyone on this side."

"Yeah," he said sleepily. "Makes it easier for us."

"No," I said. "It makes it just as bad or worse. If the klim came over, so can anything else that figures out where the breach is."

He sat up nearly as fast as I had.

"Jesus," he said. In the dim light, I saw him push a shock of hair back from his forehead.

I rubbed the sides of my face with my hands. "What do we do?"

"Stop the klim. Close the rift."

He said it like: go to the bank, then the market. Step one. Step two.

"How do we do that?"

In the silence, I listened to him breathe. Drew in the heady fragrance of his scent. Felt his mind racing, looking for a plan. Felt my own mind spin in circles.

"I have no idea," he said, "but we'll figure it out."

———

Dee had French toast and coffee on the make when I came downstairs in the morning. He nodded toward a mug he'd set out for me. "There's milk in the fridge. No sugar, but there's honey on the table if you want it."

I filled the mug with coffee and sat at the dark walnut table in one of four comfortable chairs with padded seats and backs. Sleep had helped. The klim might want to kill me, but that didn't mean it would—or could. All it meant was that we had to get it first. We might not know now how to close the rift, but we would learn.

A large window behind the table looked out into Dee's small backyard. His wizard's lair, I realized, was directly above. The backyard was landscaped and manicured like the front.

I half-wanted him to have a yard that was wild and untamed. To think that within this very in-control-of-himself man lurked a feral garden.

"How many?" he said, nodding toward the griddle.

"Two, thanks," I said.

He used a spatula to lift two pieces onto a plate, then set

the plate in front of me. He took four pieces for himself, took the chair closest to mine, and handed me a knife and fork wrapped in a napkin.

No feral garden in this man. No wild, untamed side at all.

I thought again that his need for control in his outer life was probably to balance the wildness of the magical power raging inside him. Some of which now lived in me. Maybe I'd become a neater housekeeper out of all of this.

"Good to see you smiling," he said.

Good thing he wasn't psychic, to know what I was smiling about.

"After yesterday, it feels pretty good to smile. To find things worth smiling about."

When we'd finished eating, Dee picked up his plate and mine, rinsed and washed them, and stacked them in the drain board. He came back to the table and said, "We need to formulate a plan for catching the klim, unless you already have one."

I shook my head. "I can maybe trace his signature to where he is, especially if you give me a little magical push. After that …" I turned my palms toward the sky.

"If you can find the klim, and if I can sneak up without it knowing," Dee said, "I can send it back to the Brume"

"What happens if it knows we're there?"

"Things get a lot harder. And it'll be me there, not we. If the klim is out to get you, having you near it isn't a good idea." He thought for a moment. "Can you do a location reading with a map?"

Map-based location readings involved using a small pendulum dangled over a map. The pendulum swings in the direction you need to go. Once you move the pendulum over the final destination, it swings in small circles. I'd seen friends of my parents find lost objects using the technique.

I shook my head. "It doesn't work that way for me. I have to physically follow the signature."

He pressed his lips together. I felt his thoughts churning.

"This will go faster if you let me read your thoughts while you're having them," I said. "Save you explaining whatever plans you've discarded or why you think a specific idea might work. It lets me hear the process. You might be throwing away an idea, or the spark of an idea, that we could make work if I know about it."

He went very still and said, "Just the thoughts specific to the klim, or do you get everything once you're in my mind?"

I felt how invaded my suggestion made him feel. What lurked in his very controlled mind that he didn't want me to know about?

"Everything, I'm afraid," I said. "I can't filter things to one subject and tune everything else out. It doesn't work that way."

I shrugged. "All I'm saying is, it would save time and maybe save a good idea from being thrown away."

He thought about it. "We can talk things over at the same time, right?"

"Yeah," I said. "I'll try hard to focus on just the klim, but if your thoughts skitter off in other directions, I'm going to hear that, too."

He seemed ready to say yes but snapped his fingers. He pushed back his chair and stood.

"We need to go see Sudie," he said. "Damn. I should have thought of her sooner."

"Sudie?" I said, following him as he bounded up the stairs.

"She runs the bookstore for wizards and witches on Pier," he said over his shoulder.

I knew Pier Avenue as well as I knew my own block of

the Strand. There was no occult bookstore there. I said as much.

"It's behind where the old Either/Or bookstore was. Where the Subway and the tchotchke shops are now. It takes a spell to get in. If you don't already know the bookstore is there, you'd never know it was."

"We're going to see her because ..."

He stripped off the gray T-shirt and pajama bottoms he'd slept in and started pulling on a fresh shirt and jeans. "

"If anyone would know how to close the rift, she would," he said and blew out a breath. "I need to call the office, let them know we won't be in for a while."

Dee was moving fast now—a man on a mission. Too fast for me to slow him with questions. I put on street clothes and we drove back into Hermosa Beach.

16

*W*e parked on Pier Avenue in front of the Subway. The moment I got out of the car, I felt the magic coming from the back of the building. I'd walked this block hundreds of times. Why hadn't I felt the magic before?

I followed Dee into a short, messy alleyway behind the shops. He stopped at a spot that didn't look any different from the rest of the building's back wall and muttered a spell under his breath.

I jumped back when the wall seemed to disintegrate, revealing a tiny shop filled with books, fetishes, feathers, along with boxes and bottles of who-knew-what. A large birdcage stood in front of a wide window—I couldn't figure out how there could be a window when I'd clearly seen a solid wall. From inside the cage, a mynah bird watched us with head-cocked interest.

The woman leaning on the wooden counter looked up and grinned. Slim with long, straight black hair and brown eyes, she looked at least part Asian. She wore black skinny jeans and a fuchsia T-shirt partially obscured behind a denim motorcycle-style jacket.

"Diego!" she said and held out her hands. "So good to see you."

We walked through where the wall should be and into the shop. The moment we stepped inside, the store grew in size, spreading out the whole length of the building. Dream catchers and mandalas decorated the walls. Crystal, brass, and silver wind chimes hung from the ceiling. The scent of herbs, incense, and books was heady.

"Hey, Sudie," Dee said. He took her hands in his and leaned over the counter to give her a peck on the cheek.

"And who is this?" she said, pulling her hands back and eyeing me head to toe.

I *felt* the crush she had on Dee and her assessment of me as just another in a long line of women who'd passed through his life. She was curious about me though—because Dee hadn't brought any of his women to her shop before.

He touched my shoulder and said, "This is Oona Good-light, psychic. She's learning a little magic."

Sudie held out a surprisingly long-fingered hand for as petite as she was. I blanched, as I usually did when a hand was extended to me. It's normally so quick the other person doesn't catch it.

But Sudie said, "Touch psychic, yeah? I have a friend in Chicago who's the same way. Hates shaking hands. Won't even go to the mall for fear of bumping into a stranger and being flooded with too much information."

"I don't mind," I said and shook hands with her, even holding on a moment longer than I wanted to, just to be polite.

"Should *I* mind?" Sudie said. "All my secrets revealed to you in an instant?"

A few things had been revealed—not just her intense crush on Dee, but that she was annoyed with her roommate for letting Sudie's cat out the back door again, and that she had a dentist appointment that afternoon she was dreading. And that the two things she wanted most in life were for someone to love her dearly and to be a help to the magic community. I could appreciate both desires.

"Not at all," I lied. "I have to turn on the psychic stuff for it to work. Your secrets are safe from me."

She gave me a look that said she didn't believe that for an instant but was willing to let it go.

She turned her gaze to Diego. "What can I do for you today?"

"I need something special," he said. "A spell to seal a breach between worlds."

Sudie's eyes widened. "What?"

"There's a breach between our world and the Brume. Something has already crossed over. Oona and I will take care of sending it back, but I need a spell to make sure neither it, nor anything else, can come over again."

"What came over?" Sudie's voice was a whisper.

"A klimertin. A klim. Oona drew a picture of what she *saw*. Maurice identified it."

"I've never heard of that," she said, 'but Maurice knows his stuff. If he says it's this klim thing, then it is." She lifted her long black hair off her neck and then let it fall back into place. "What's it doing here?"

"It was hungry. It feeds off negative emotion—anger, fear, jealousy, and the like. It's getting people to murder their closest friends and devouring the emotions."

"Holy shit," she said. Her face grew thoughtful. "That's going to take some research. I know there is a way. Give me a day to dig through the books."

"Give me a call if you find anything," he said.

Sudie nodded and said something under her breath. A sudden breeze cooled my back. I turned and saw the wall had dissolved again.

"I'll call," she said behind us as we walked out into the crisp, autumn day.

We were getting into Dee's car when a little brown and gray house sparrow darted in before he completely shut his door. I leaned back in the seat, startled. The bird perched on the steering wheel and turned its head, looking first at Dee, then me, then back at Dee.

"What's up?" Dee said to the bird. "Did Sudie think of something?"

The bird nodded its head and chirped.

"Okay. Thanks." He opened the car door wide. The bird took wing and was gone in an instant.

"Sudie wants us back in the store," he said.

"Yeah. I got that."

He laughed. "The look on your face—"

"You magic folk." I shook my head.

We made our way back toward the short alley again.

"I thought you had mages in your family," Dee said as we turned the corner and I looked again at the building's seeming blank back wall.

"Ancestors," I said. "My mother's gift is healing. She does it by touch. She has a few shifters as patients, so I know about that, and a few wizards and witches as friends, but as a kid I hardly paid any attention to them; they were my parents' friends and it wasn't like they sat around conjuring puppies and ponies in the living room. My parents had lots of non-magical friends, too, some of whom I now realize were famous in their fields. They were just Mr. or Ms. So-and-so to me. I guess I was pretty self-absorbed as a kid."

"Self-absorbed or self-protective?" Dee said.

I frowned. "Some of both, I guess. I've been over-whelmed by others' thoughts and emotions for as long as I can remember. I've always been a bit of a recluse. Being plunged into all this magic is …" I didn't know what word to use. Weird? Exhilarating? Scary? Fascinating? "It's a constant surprise."

"I grew up in a commune," Dee said. "Five families living together, practicing their arts together, raising and homeschooling us kids in the ways of magic together. This world is my normal. The only time I mixed with anyone not magical was at hockey."

I took that in. Dee hardly ever spoke about his family or his history. Those few words probably tripled what I knew about him outside of direct experience. It was funny how our lives seemed almost to be mirror images—he was raised in magic; my parents sought to make my childhood as ordinary and non-magical as possible. He only mixed with the non-magical through sports; I only mixed with the magical through my mother's patients and a few of my parents' close friends. He took the magical world for granted; I found it strange—equally as exotic and tempting as it was weird and frightening.

He muttered the spell to open Sudie's door.

"I've got it," Sudie said as soon as we came inside. A large book lay open in front of her on the counter. "I'm glad the sparrow caught you. I think I've got the spell you need."

The mynah bird that had been silent while we'd been in the shop earlier now said, "I helped."

"Major did help," Sudie said. "He reminded me about an old book I had in the back room. He said the answer was in there. I already knew about the spell, but it had slipped my mind until he mentioned the book."

"What sort of spell?" Dee said.

"A mending spell. For fixing big rifts. Multigenerational family feuds. Countries after war. That sort of thing. I'm pretty sure it will mend the rift between the worlds."

"Pretty sure?"

She shrugged. "Any spell being used for a new purpose, you never know how well it will work until you try it."

Dee didn't look convinced.

"Take a look at it," she said.

Sudie rotated the book around so that the text was right side up for him. Dee bent forward and read.

"This spell needs a tool to make it work," he said, looking up from the book.

Sudie grinned. "Fortunately for you, I happen to have a mending orb."

She reached under the counter and then handed something to him. He rotated his wrist so his palm was up and opened his hand to show me what she'd given him.

The orb looked like a pigeon egg-sized ruby ground into a perfect sphere.

Dee shivered and passed the orb from his right to left hand and back again.

Sudie laughed. "Jam-packed with magic, isn't it? I could barely hold the orb long enough to carry it out from the back room." She reached under the counter again. "Here." She handed him a small, blue velvet sack with runes stitched on it in gold thread.

Dee dropped the orb inside and tugged the drawstrings closed.

Sudie set her hand on the opened book's page. "Do you want me to make a copy of the spell for you?"

Dee shook his head. "I've got it."

"Of course you do." She looked at me. "Did you know

Diego has a photographic memory? Really useful for a wizard."

I nodded, but my thoughts weren't on Dee's seemingly endless bag of tricks. I was focused on the spell and the orb. Wondering how we were going to get the klim back into its own world and hold it there—and hold off all the other things that lived there—while we stitched up the rift.

And once that was done, how were we going to get back?

17

*B*ack in Dee's car again, he said, "I'm famished. How about Good Stuff for breakfast?"

I blinked, confused by his change of attitude. "I thought you said you didn't want me out in public any more than necessary?"

He half-shrugged. "Things have changed. We need to draw out the klim now. Bring it to us."

"So, we're going to dangle me as bait?"

"You can say no."

He didn't say it like a challenge. I took it that way, though.

"Yeah," I said. "Fine. Let's get this bastard."

We parked on the second level of the parking structure at Thirteenth. When we reached the street, Dee took my hand. I shot him a look.

"Just a normal couple out for breakfast," he said and smiled. "Nothing to see here."

"The klim won't be fooled," I said. "It feeds off emotions. Real emotions. It won't buy some fakery."

"Is it fake, Oona?" he said. "There seems to be some spark between us."

I spotted an open table on the Good Stuff patio and motioned toward it with my head. I liked sitting in the patio, only a short wall of separation between us diners and folks out to enjoy the beach. I liked watching the people strolling, rollerblading, skateboarding, biking by in the sunshine.

People watching counted as safe social interaction for me. No one touched me. If I was lucky, no one talked to me. For the most part, the emotions swirling around and poking at my consciousness this morning were positive.

Except Dee was still touching me. Not physically now, but his question jabbed like a feather—not painful but insistent. *Answer the question: is it fake?*

"We hardly know each other," I said as I sat.

He smiled and settled in the chair on the other side of the small table. "And yet you've given me a pet name. Do you always give pet names to people you hardly know and have no feelings for?"

"Do you always fall in love so quickly?"

He stiffened. "I never said love." He leaned toward me, the momentary tension gone. "Lust, though. Lots of lust. Respect. Trust. Caring. Didn't you hear what Maurice said? The more you deny you're as interested as I am in seeing where this goes, the more the klim laps up your conflicted feelings. Do you really want to give it that fuel?"

His words struck me hard. The last thing I wanted to do was feed the klim. But he was right that my feelings toward, and about, him were conflicted. But then, I was conflicted about most things. Did I love being psychic or wish it would go away so I wouldn't have to hear people's thoughts and feel their emotions? I loved my self-exiled solitary life and yet longed to be out in the world with a gaggle of companions. I

146

liked having only a few close friends, and wished my phone rang more often.

At some point I was going to have to make up my mind about a boatload of things and commit to the choices.

But not right now. The skin between my shoulder blades was prickling.

I grabbed Dee's hand. "The klim is around here somewhere. I've caught its signature."

My gaze darted to the Strand. The klim could be any of the people there. Good Stuff was on a busy corner. People coming to or leaving the beach walked by almost constantly. People who'd parked in the structure or on the street paraded down to the sand. The klim could be among them. Was among them—somewhere.

A group of women with young children passed by us, followed closely by a woman who seemed to be both with, and not with, them. The straggler woman stopped in front of our table, bent, and picked up something from the street.

"You dropped this," she said, and handed me a small rectangle of paper. I dropped it on the table and looked down at it. A business card. When I glanced back up, the woman was no longer with the group of mothers and children.

Dee, his eyes narrowed, watched the small group walk away from the beach toward Hermosa Avenue. He moved his gaze to me.

"What did the klim bring us?"

"You caught that, too," I said.

"I watched it change from the woman who handed you the paper to some sort of weird lizard-crab thing. Something small that I couldn't keep my eye on as it scuttled away." He rolled his shoulders. "I've seen shifting before, but not into something I'm pretty sure is not of our world. And the clothes

147

went with it. Except for fairies, I've never known a shifter who didn't have to get naked to change."

A shiver ran down my spine. "The klim's signature is confused—coming from somewhere nearby, and from this." I glanced down at the business card. "I can't get a fix on location." I picked up the card and looked at it. Jeremy Collins, it read in a bold font. Below that: Stockbroker. And below that, an address in Redondo Beach and a 310 phone number. I handed the card to Dee.

"We have to go to this place," I said, standing so quickly I almost knocked over my chair. "This man's in danger."

Dee laid his hand on my arm. "Feel it out, Oona. Does it feel like a trap?"

I let out a long breath. He had a point. I'd caught the klim's signature and followed it to the man it had killed in Redondo Beach. The klim straight out giving us an address and pretty much leading us by the nose was new. I closed my eyes and felt for intent, but of course I couldn't read the klim's mind any better today than on any past day. I closed my hand around the business card and felt for the man whose name it bore.

"I feel danger around this Jeremy Collins but to him, not to us. We have to hurry."

He nodded and stood. The waitress had already brought two waters but hadn't taken our order yet. Dee tucked a ten under the small ceramic container that held sugars and other sweeteners, and we left.

I put the address into the map app on my phone.

"North Redondo," I said. "Almost into Torrance. Off Artesia Boulevard."

I turned up the phone's volume for the turn-by-turn directions. My stomach cramped harder the closer we came to our destination. There was a chance the klim was sending us off on a wild goose chase for reasons of its own, and a slim chance there wouldn't be a dead body at the end, but I doubted it. Dee's tension rolled off him in waves, multiplying my own anxiety. By the time we pulled up to a three story, blue stucco office building, my heart was beating hard and my throat was dry.

"Suite 201," I said, glancing down at the business card.

"What do you feel?" Dee said.

My nerves were tight as bowstrings. A tension headache beat against the inside of my skull.

"Nothing good," I said.

We ran up the stairs to the second floor and found Suite 201. A small brass plaque read *Collins and Steinman*. No designation of what sort of business it was, but stockbroker written on Jeremy Collins' business card gave a pretty good hint.

The door to the suite was locked.

I glanced at my phone to see the time. "Out on lunch break?"

Dee ran his hand over his hair. "If something has happened to this Jeremy Collins, we'll have to be out of here before anyone gets back."

"Is it still breaking and entering if you use magic to open the door?" I said.

Dee glanced at me. "Yeah. It is."

I hiked up a tensed shoulder in a tense shrug.

He drew in a short breath and muttered a spell. I heard a click. Dee took hold of the knob and opened the door.

The empty reception area wasn't large, but the reception-ist's desk and the visitors' chairs were tasteful and looked expensive. Off the reception area were two closed doors. My throat was so dry, I half-looked around, hoping for a fridge with bottled water or something.

Dee nudged me with his elbow and looked toward one of the closed doors A thin, rectangular brass plaque on it read *Jeremy Collins*.

I shook my head. I didn't want to see behind that door. Violence had been done here. The residue floated in the air like ash.

Dee tried the door. Locked. He muttered something, and the lock clicked. He grabbed the knob and pushed the door open.

Blood was everywhere. Red splatter clung to the walls. Red—and gray. Bits of brain matter. Red pools soaked the carpeting. A bloody baseball bat lay next to the destroyed body. The blood on it was dry. The klim had killed him and then sought us out. I turned and ran from the room.

I was bent over, my hands braced on my knees, breathing hard when Dee followed me out into the reception area.

"You okay?" he said.

I shook my head no. "I need to get out of here."

"Come on." He took hold of my upper arm, gently got me standing up straight again, and helped me out the door.

"We have to call the police," I said once we were in the hallway.

"In the car," he said.

He held onto me as we descended the stairs. My knees were wobbly. I wasn't sure I would have made it without stumbling.

I'd seen more dead bodies in the last nine days than in my whole life.

In the car, Dee opened the glove box and pulled out a cheap pay-as-you-go cell phone. He called 911 and reported a dead person at the address, gave a fake name and other information. When he was done, he put the cell phone under the front tire and ran over it as we drove away.

"What was the thing with the phone about?" I said as we headed west on Artesia Boulevard, back toward the beach. My head was throbbing. I wanted to be back in my own house, but we were safer at Dee's.

"The cops will find the phone. They won't waste time looking for it or trying to trace the call," he said. "Hopefully they won't look for the caller, either."

"So we don't have to explain how we got into an inner office to find the body. Or why we were there at all."

Dee nodded. "The magic police—that's a different matter."

"Magic police?"

"They can take a dim view of using magic to break into an office."

"Back up," I said. "Magic police?"

He turned right on Sepulveda, heading back toward his house. "You don't know about them? Your parents really did keep you in the ordinary world, didn't they? The MPs are like the regular cops except that they deal with anyone and anything magical."

"Do they know about the klim?"

He nodded. "I have a friend on the force, Jack. I've kept him updated with everything we've learned."

"So, they're looking for the klim too?"

He shrugged. "Jack is."

"What does that mean?"

"That means that the MPs are sometimes more interested in enforcing rules than actually catching bad guys."

"Like using magic to break into a locked office."

"Mmm," Dee said. "It drives Jack nuts. Even if the MPs caught the klim and banished it back to the Brume, healing the rift isn't in their purview. That's going to be up to us, as far as I can see."

I was okay with that. It was me the klim wanted to kill. And even though going into the Brume for real and trying to close the rift made my heart pound with fear, it was the only way to be personally sure the klim couldn't come after me again.

18

J sat at Dee's kitchen table looking into his manicured backyard but seeing Jeremy Collins broken body in my mind's eye.

Dee handed me a mug of tea. I sniffed the brew and wondered if he'd made it from ingredients in his kitchen or in his lair. Either was okay. I just liked to know what I was drinking.

"What is this?" I said.

"Soothing herbs. Chamomile. Lavender. Verbena. Lemon balm. You've been trembling ever since we found the stock-broker's body."

"Jeremy Collins," I said, wanting him to have a name, not just an occupation.

"Jeremy. Yeah."

I took a sip from the mug. The tea felt good going down. Warm. I looked at him sitting across the table from me, both hands wrapped around his own mug.

"It's too much death, Dee."

"I know."

He did know. I saw it in his face, *felt* it in him. If we

weren't careful, we would go down the rabbit hole of shock and sorrow, fall into that place where everything seemed pointless and nothing seemed worth the effort anymore.

"It hurts, Dee, it hurts my soul."

"Their pain is your pain," he said. "Of course it's hard."

I turned the mug in my hands and stared into its depths. I craved that psychic filter Dee had told me about, but it seemed as out of reach as a star. I'd needed refuge from the world when the worst assault on my psyche was everyday people and their everyday lives. Brad's death. Eric's. The man in Redondo. Jeremy. Every death senseless. Useless. Every death as painful as a shot to the heart for me.

"How do you stand it?" I said. "I want to go home, barricade myself behind the door and never come out."

"It's not always like this," he said. "It's *never* been like this. But my job, the work I do, the work *we* are doing now, it's about trying to set things right. It's worth going for the win."

"Goalie," I said more to myself than him. "Last chance for the save."

"You don't seem the kind to give up on the play," he said.

"I can be," I said, "when I'm exhausted, like now. When I feel I'm trying to play way over my level and there's no way I can even compete, much less contribute to the win."

"You're not over your level. You're completely in the mix, right where you belong."

I set down the mug and wrapped my arms across my body. If I was where I belonged, why did I desperately want to pack up and go home, my head hung in defeat?

"I can't bring Brad or Eric or Jeremy back to life," I said. "Back to their families."

"You can help stop the klim from hurting anyone else," Dee said. "That's important. That'd be a huge win."

I sniffed and nodded.

He stood. "Come on."

"Where are we going?"

"Upstairs," he said. "It's been a hellacious day. A nap, a rest, whatever, would do us both good."

"Do you have music up there?" I asked, following him up the stairs. "I could do with some music."

He looked over his shoulder at me. "No." He grinned. "But I could sing to you."

I managed a thin smile. "Dear Lord. Anything but that."

His bed was still unmade from this morning. He straightened the covers and we lay down on top them. He slipped an arm under my shoulders and pulled me close to him.

His scent filled my nose. His heartbeat was slow. Steady. Comforting. We lay quietly long enough that I wondered if he'd fallen asleep.

Sleep would have been welcome, but I knew it was impossible for me. Too much circled in my head. The dead. The klim. The Brume. It left me feeling helpless. Sad. Alone.

I didn't want to feel alone. I needed that fine medicine of total, deep human contact. I shifted position and kissed Dee's chest.

It wasn't right to ask for the comfort of his body to ease the despair that threatened to drown me. Wasn't fair to want from him what I didn't want him asking of me.

But I wanted—needed—more than the sound of his heartbeat to drive back the creeping dark. I needed his passion. Our life forces raging, merged. The ultimate affirmation.

He opened his eyes slowly.

"Dee," I said, and *felt* his needs, as desperate as my own.

He rolled over to face me and kissed the side of my neck. And then the hollow of my throat. He undid the first button of my shirt. And the second.

The day was sunny, bright. Outside, birds chattered in the trees. Inside, my heart banged in my chest. It's been a long time since I'd been with anyone. I'd never been with anyone whose touch felt as good to me as his did. He wanted things from me—every man I'd ever been with wanted something—but Dee's wants were different. Trust. Partnership. Sex to seal the bond.

Death had brought me this sudden desire. Death and the desperate need of life to oppose it. I knew it but knowing didn't counter needing him now like a drowning woman needed air. I guessed I wasn't conflicted anymore.

He helped me out of my clothes, took off his own, and lay next to me again.

I traced the symbols that ran from his shoulder to his wrist. He'd taught me their meanings: Strength. Protection. Heart. Mind. Spirit. A small candle with a tall flame to honor his mother's magic. A triquetra woven around a circle in honor of his father's. Magic inked into his skin. Other symbols circled each of his ankles—the four elements, light and dark, life and death in an endless circle.

"We should get you some," he said. "To keep you safe."

I nodded. I would have agreed to anything he said at that moment if he'd just—please—just—

We clung to each other then. Me pressing into him. Him pressing into me. Our skins learning the other.

Until something switched, and we were everywhere with hands, mouths, lips, teeth—our breaths coming in gasps. I *felt* him wanting, needing, wondering, waiting for the right moment.

Now, I wanted to scream. But it seemed he knew better than I did, stroking, teasing, pleasing until I did scream. And he tensed, his eyes squeezed shut, and surrendered everything he was to me, as I had to him.

After, we lay together, spent.

He pushed a strand of hair away from my face and kissed the side of my mouth. "Damn, woman," he whispered. "It's never been like that. Never."

"Heady stuff," I said.

"Yeah." He laughed then, low and throaty. Filled with joy.

Laughter burbled out of me like bubbles from a child's pipe. We wrapped our arms around each other and rolled around the bed, our laughter growing until I felt tears in my eyes.

I pulled one arm free and waved my hand in front of my face, fanning away the tears.

"I need to pee," I said, half-apologizing for my biological needs.

He grinned, fell back hard against a pillow, and waved me off toward the bathroom.

When I came back, he'd pulled on a pair of jeans.

"Done with me already?" I said lightly.

"Just getting started," he said. "But I was serious before, about getting some protection on your skin. We're contemplating going into the Brume together, not a vision but actually going. We're both going to need to take with us all the magic and power we can."

Now that the madness of passion had died down, the reality of the klim and all the rest flooded back. Brad's, Eric's, and Jeremy's families would never have the satisfaction of knowing what had killed their loved ones, but maybe we could stop the klim from hurting anyone else. Maybe that had to be enough.

"It doesn't hurt," he said about the tattoo. "Not so much that you'd pass out, at least."

"That's very comforting," I said, pulling on my shirt and doing up the buttons.

Dee put his arms around me, bent me back in an old-fashioned swoon and gave me a long, deep kiss. He brought me back upright and said, "Come on. Gill locks up at six pm sharp on Tuesdays and The Gate usually leaves earlier."

"The Gate?"

Dee pulled on a navy T-shirt and dropped to one knee to tie his white running shoes. "I suppose the old man has an actual name, but he's The Gate to everyone. You have to be approved by him before Gill does the ink."

"What if he doesn't approve me?"

"It's happened." He patted his pockets, checking he had everything he needed. "We'll go and see what he says."

I expected Gill's place to be like Sudie's, hidden from the ordinary world. Instead, Dee parked in front of a large, well-lit tattoo parlor on Hermosa Avenue and said, "Here we are. Still nervous?"

I nodded. "I have this thing about needles. And pain. Not a fan of either."

We got out of the car and he took my hand. "It's not that bad. I promise."

I drew in a deep breath and we walked into the shop.

The man behind the long black counter looked up as we walked in. He was around Dee's age, late twenties, I guessed, tallish, with sandy-brown hair and bright green eyes. Honestly, was every magical man handsome beyond the bounds of normality?

I glanced around the shop. Four green faux-leather and chrome chairs were pushed up against the street-side wall. Four thick black binders lay on a coffee table in front of the chairs. The beige walls had sheets of paper with drawings of available tattoos randomly Scotch-taped on them. The air had a slightly medicinal smell.

The man—Gill, I assumed—grinned when he saw Dee

and came around from behind the counter. The two men clasped hands and then drew each other into a tight bro hug.

"Long time," Gill said, turning Dee loose. "How've you been? How's the ink holding up?"

"I've been good, and you know your ink never fades or fails. How have you been?"

"No complaints," Gill said, and then eyed me, curiosity plain on his face.

"This is Oona," Dee said. "Oona, meet Gill—best tattoo artist in the western hemisphere."

Gill smiled. "You are too kind. Are you here for yourself or the lady today?"

"For Oona. Something for protection from beasts of the Brume."

Gill's eyes opened wide. I *felt* him simultaneously scanning me for something and worrying over what Dee had said. I *felt* him decide I was okay, or worthy, or whatever, and shift his concerns completely to the Brume.

"Do you know what a klim is?" Dee asked him.

Gil nodded and muttered, "Bad shit."

"Yeah," Dee said. "There's one here. Came through a rift between worlds. It's got a thing for Oona."

Gil tugged at a lock of his hair that had fallen over his forehead. "You need to talk to The Gate. He's in back."

I followed Dee through a hanging black curtain, past the chairs and massage-type tables for customers, past the small tables with tattoo guns at the ready and drawers full of inks, down a narrow hall to a small office. The door was open, and we walked in. The magic in the room roiled over me like floodwaters. I grabbed Dee's arm to steady myself, and then let go—determined to find my balance myself.

The office held an old, scarred wooden desk and chair, three small visitor chairs, and some large pillows on the floor.

The walls were painted black and covered in glowing signs and runes. It was a stark contrast to the light, cheerful front workspace—and a little creepy.

The Gate was nowhere to be seen.

Dee settled into one of the chairs and nodded for me to take another. I lifted my eyebrows at him in question.

"He's here," Dee said. "He likes to observe new people before he meets them. Wants to know if you sweat."

Which, now that I knew, I refused to do. There was a stubborn streak in me that rose up at the oddest times. Likely enough it was just another way of protecting myself, but it worked. I took a breath in, let it out, relaxed, and smiled at Dee. I let my gaze wander around the room again, trying to read the runes.

I spotted one I recognized as a match to a tattoo on Dee's arm. The sign for strength. I found earth and air nearby. As I watched, the runes slowly changed, morphing into something entirely different. Where the rune for water had been, now was the rune for life. I wondered if The Gate was trying to say something or just messing with me.

A hidden door behind the desk opened and an older man who must have been drop-dead handsome in his youth—what was it with these magical men?—walked in. His hair was silver and grey, cut short on the sides but longish on top and worn swept back from his forehead. He was a bit stocky, but looked good in the black trousers, button-down gray shirt, and polished black Florsheims he wore. Hand him a briefcase and he easily could be pegged for a lawyer or senior executive in some large corporation.

Dee rose to his feet and made a small bow. "Sir."

The Gate smiled broadly and threw open his arms. "Diego! How wonderful to see you." The two men embraced, then broke apart. The Gate took the chair behind the desk. Then Dee sat back down.

"The Gate was my mentor," Dee said, his gaze on the man.

My eyes widened. The man with the psychic niece. The one who might be able to tell me how to build a filter for myself.

The older man laughed. "You know, usually a wizard of his level kills his mentor when he's gotten all he can from him. The wizard kills the mentor and steals his magic. It's sort of a Rite of Passage. Either Diego feels there is still more I can teach him, or he just hasn't gotten around to dispatching me yet."

My gaze flickered from one to the other.

"I'll never know everything you have to teach," Dee said quietly, and with clear affection in his voice. "I think you're safe for a while more."

The Gate smiled, then turned his attention to me. I *felt* him examine me, searching my core, peering into my soul. My throat felt dry, my hands clammy. So much for my stubborn streak keeping me calm and strong. I forced myself not to turn away from his gaze.

"Artist," he said, as though having discovered something delightful. He broke his bond with me and rummaged in a desk drawer. He drew out a stubby Number Two pencil and a 5x7 pad of blank paper. He held both out to me. "Draw something."

"What kind of something?" I said.

The Gate gave a wildly exaggerated shrug. "You choose."

Great. Dee seemed to think the tattoo was important and the man who would decide if I'd get one or not had just basically commanded me to draw. It was pretty clear that what I drew would influence his decision. No pressure.

I took the pencil and pad and let my mind go blank. I closed my eyes and drew. When I opened my eyes, I saw I'd drawn a stylized eagle. I didn't know where that had come from. I didn't usually draw birds.

The Gate clapped his hands, evidently pleased with what my subconscious had come up with. Dee, I noticed, glanced away.

"What?" I said.

The Gate wiggled his finger between us, indicating us both. "So, you two? Recently?"

Dee shrugged. "Today. First time."

"Ah," The Gate said. "That helps explain it. 'Course it's not just the sex she's responding to. Things are a little deeper than that."

I felt my annoyance rising. These two were talking around me and I resented it.

The Gate grinned. "The eagle is associated with Saint Juan Diego. Close enough on the name, don't you think? The saint's original Indian name, Cuauhtlatoatzin, meant white eagle, or eagle who speaks. This drawing will be your mark. The eagle will always be with you and will provide strength when you need it. Gil will put sunrays behind it, in honor to masculine power. Don't worry. It will be small and discrete."

I looked at Dee and shrugged. I liked the drawing. I even liked the idea of it.

The Gate turned his attention to him. "*She* is your protector, you know." The older man grinned again. He was having an awful lot of fun.

"So," The Gate said to Dee, "a new tattoo for you as well, Diego. What shall it be, to seal your connection with this fierce lamb?" He tapped his index finger against his chin while he thought.

"Got it," he said. "For you, the numeral one, for Oona, and the moon, for her feminine power and grace."

He turned his sights on me. "Draw," he said, as though it were an invitation, not a command.

I didn't want to do it. Didn't want to permanently stick Dee with some sketch of mine on his skin. But he leaned forward, interested to see what I'd come up with.

Dee's skin was so busy with signs and symbols, I wanted to give him something simple and clean. I drew a numeral 1 embraced by a crescent moon.

"Sweet," he said.

The Gate stood, and Dee immediately came to his feet as well. I stood, too. It seemed the thing to do.

"Gil will take care of you," The Gate said.

He turned as if to leave, but I said, "Excuse me. Can I ask a question?"

The Gate turned back and locked his eyes on mine.

My throat felt dry. I cleared it and said, "Diego told me your niece is a psychic. That she found a way to build a defense around herself so that the wants and needs of everyone around her didn't prick at her constantly."

The Gate raised his eyebrows slightly but didn't break his tight gaze on me.

"Do you know how she did it? Could you tell me?"

The desperation in my voice was pitiful. I watched him, my heart beating, waiting for his reply.

His gaze never wavered.

"No," he said.

My heart sank.

He turned again, pulled open the disguised door and vanished behind it.

I stared after him and forced back the whimper that rose in my throat.

Dee tapped me with his elbow. "That's just the way he is."

A fact that offered absolutely no comfort.

"Does he ever change his mind?"

He shook his head. "Never. But, you asked two questions. His no could have been directed at both or only one of them. And there's always the chance that yes is the answer to a slightly different question."

I shook out my hands, like shaking off water, trying to drive away my nerves and frustrations. It sort of worked.

"He was your teacher?" I said.

Dee nodded. "My father sent me to him when I was sixteen. Gil had come six months earlier. We were his only two apprentices until I left when I turned twenty-one."

"Did he make you nuts?"

Dee laughed once. "Oh, yeah."

"But you respect him."

Dee shrugged. "That, too." He nudged me again. "Come on. Let's go see Gil."

An hour later, we walked out of the shop, each with a fresh piece of plastic wrap over our new tattoos. The process hadn't hurt as much as I'd feared it would. The Gate intoning over me while Gil inked the stylized eagle within a sunburst on my upper arm helped take my mind off the reality of the needle.

It was both weird and weirdly moving. Another weird thing was that as the eagle was going on, I felt a growing physical connection to Dee, binding us together.

When Gil finished with me, I watched my drawing be transferred onto Dee. One good thing about being psychic, you never have to guess whether someone is really pleased or simply being polite. Dee was truly pleased with the design.

By the time we left, the sun was sinking toward the sea,

the sky aflame with streaks of pink, purple, yellow, and blue —and we were suddenly and completely spent.

Over dinner at his house, I had to ask, "Maurice and The Gate seemed awfully interested in our sex life."

Dee blanched slightly and glanced down at the tabletop. He looked up again. "In magic, sex is pretty important. It's a source of power. The more sex a wizard has, the more recent the sex, the more powerful they are."

I stared at him. "I gather you're pretty a powerful wizard."

Dee shrugged. I could see how uncomfortable he was.

"So ..." I let the question hang in the air.

The walls and ceiling suddenly seemed to fascinate him, judging by how his gaze slid over them.

"Yeah," he said, still not looking at me. "Lots of experience. Lots of partners."

Not news I wanted to hear, but not all that surprising either.

"Condoms?" Because when you have sex with someone, you're basically having sex with everyone they've ever been with and whatever little surprises might have been left behind, unless protection was used.

He turned his gaze back to me. "Not necessary because —magic."

"Seriously?"

"The ultimate in safe sex," he said. "Magic folk hardly ever catch colds or get the flu, either. We don't get serious diseases or dotty in our old age. Well, in The Gate's case, maybe a little dotty."

My mother had magical patients but, thinking back, not one came in because of illness, only for injuries. My own ancestors, from Audrey on, had lived long, healthy lives. I'd put it down to luck and good genes.

"Okay," I said, not at all sure how I felt about his history or the whole sex generating magical power thing. Was it me Dee made love to—Oona Goodlight, person—or miscellaneous female, power generator? I was tempted to slip into his thoughts and find out.

I settled for the look on his face and his evident hesitancy to discuss the subject. I chose to believe he wasn't a jerk. We all came with the past we'd lived. All that mattered was how we lived going forward.

When we finished eating Dee picked up the dishes and washed them. I dried. I would have been willing to bet that his dishwasher had never been used. Mine served as an extra cupboard—stacking in the dishes until there were enough to run a load and pulling clean dishes out as I needed them until the dishwasher was empty. Then the cycle started over.

For dessert, we made love slowly, neither of us up for the mad passions of our first time. I was sure now it was *me* he made love to. No man wanting a quick jolt of power and nothing more could fake that kind of tender exploration. After, I fell into the sort of sleep that only comes from deep contentment. Evidently Dee wasn't the only one who could compartmentalize life's contradictory facets.

19

I woke with a start, drenched in sweat and breathing hard. I sat up in Dee's bed and stared into the darkness.

He set his hand on my back. "What's wrong?"

I rubbed the side of my face and tried to steady my breath. "I had a terrible dream about Jeremy Collins. He wanted to be with his family. He thought I was keeping him from them."

Dee sat up next to me.

"Christ, Dee. Is it always like this for you—beasts from the Brume inciting murder and dreams of dead stockbrokers demanding their families? Is your life spent being chased by evil while trying to beat back death and sorrow? Because I can't take a lot of this."

He put his arm over my shoulders and tried to draw me close to him. I shrugged his arm away and sat straight.

"I told you before," he said, "it's never been like this. But it is this way now. We have work to do and getting upset up over the horrible things that have happened doesn't get us any closer to getting it done." His voice dropped low. "If you want, I'll take you home right now, set up wards that I'm sure no one and nothing can get through, and you can just ride it out until you're safe again."

I glared at him. "That's what you think? That I want to go home and hide while you do the dirty work? If that were the case, I'd have said, 'Let's turn this whole thing over to the Magic Police and be done with it.' But I didn't say that, did I?"

He smiled. "Nope." He laid his arm around my shoulders again and this time I didn't pull away.

"I'm in," I said. "But when this is over, I don't want to do this anymore."

I sidled out of his arms and off the bed. I put my hands on my hips and stretched the tension-stiffened muscles in my back. "It'll be dawn soon. We still need a plan for catching the klim and sending it back"

"That part's easy. I have an elegant spell that will send it back to the Brume. I'll teach it to you. Two voices are stronger than one, especially in this case."

He drew in a deep breath and I knew something else was coming.

"The hard part," he said, "is that the klim has to be close enough to hear the words, and for one, or both of us, to pour an elixir on its skin."

"Getting within shouting distance isn't close enough?"

"Sorry," he said. "But neither of us have to actually touch it. Close enough to wet it with the elixir will do fine."

"Small favors," I said, making light while my stomach tightened. "So, the klim goes back to the Brume. Then what?"

"We follow it in and stitch up the rift the klim came through, using the spell Sudie found and the healing orb."

Dee had this habit of making things sound like they were going to be a lot easier than I knew they'd turn out to be.

I dry-ran some possible scenarios in my head.

"We can't confront the klim in public," I said. "Even if it looks human, we can't be spouting enchantments and throwing elixir at someone in front of a bunch of people. And what happens when people see this 'person' disappear as the klim is returned to the Brume?"

"Do you have an alternative?" he said.

I pressed my lips together. I had one, but I didn't like it.

"We have to get the klim into a private space," I said. "Somewhere we can be sure no passing person will wander in."

Dee sat up on the edge of the bed, leaned forward and tucked his hands between his knees. "Where?"

I scratched my neck. "Your house. Or mine."

I *felt* his abhorrence of the idea of having the klim in his house. His emotion wasn't anywhere close to the strength of mine, though. I loved my home. The Goodlight House. It was my castle and my sanctuary. A very private sanctuary. The idea of drawing the klim inside it made me sick.

Dee sat very still for a long moment. I could practically see the gears turning in his head as he looked for an alternative. I watched the shift on his face when he realized there wasn't one.

Wednesday morning, we sat in front of my house on the short concrete wall that separated the sand from the Strand. Dee looked calm and happy. The weather was cool. He wore tan cargo pants and a light jacket over his T-shirt.

I had on a pair of his cargo pants—for the pockets, and my favorite shirt—for luck, a gray hoodie, and hiking boots. I tried to get that 'great autumn day at the beach' look going on my face but wasn't succeeding too well. My guts were churning. My hand kept straying to where, under my shirt and hoodie, the new tattoo on my upper arm seemed to tingle. My gaze strayed to where I knew the new one Dee wore lay hidden under his shirt. Magic, I trusted, would protect us from the klim and anything we'd run into in the Brume.

But when I said as much to Dee, he said, "The ink offers some protection, but it's not a repellent. Don't count on mere magic to keep you safe."

Mere magic?

"What do I count on then?"

"Me. Same as I'll rely on you." He gave me a humorless smile. "Don't let me down."

"You're nervous too," I said, feeling it suddenly rise in him like steam. He stared out across the sand to the ocean without speaking. I felt him will his nervousness away.

"Cautious," he said, looking at me again. "Busy trying to think through possibilities for a situation that's impossible to predict. It's futile but feels better than sitting here just waiting. And much better than getting freaked out."

"Sheesh," I said lightly. "Here you go getting all wise on me again."

The back of my neck prickled. A small ache began inching its way up my skull. Dee started to say something, but I cut him off.

"It's nearby," I said in a whisper. A normal tone seemed wrong—as if the klim might hear us even though I knew it wasn't close enough to hear my words unless it had the hearing of an owl.

"Where?" Dee said, casually turning his head left and right.

"Down a ways. A few blocks south of the pier. Going north. Moving away from us."

Without Dee's elixir, I couldn't read the klim's thoughts, but counting on the extra magic Dee had given me, I tried to *feel* it.

The beast's emotions blasted over me. Desperation. Hunger. Hatred.

I *felt* the beast calculating.

Hunting.

We had to make the klim turn around. Catch our psychic scents. Come to us.

"Dee," I said.

He swung his head to look at me, alarmed by my tone.

I leaned close to him. "I have to tell you now. Before anything happens and I don't get the chance later. I love you, Diego Adair. Deeply."

My heart pounded. My mouth went dry. I wanted to take back the words the moment I'd said them. What was wrong with me that I'd say such a thing?

Shit. Shit. Shit.

But I had to get a rise out of him. Generate strong emotions from both of us. Strong enough that the klim couldn't resist. That he'd hunt us down to feed on all that we felt. That it would realize I was close and come for me.

Emotions radiated from Dee like solar flares. Surprise. Pleasure. Confusion. Fear. Disbelief.

And from me—shame. That I'd lied about something so important.

Except, I realized, it was maybe a little true.

And that kicked off a whole new set of feelings cascading through me. If the klim liked the taste of my conflicted emotions, I was offering him a feast—and myself. The klim wanted its revenge—me, dead. All it had to do was come and get me.

I grabbed Dee's arm. "It's caught our scent. It's moving this way."

All I had to do was figure out which of the many people heading our way was the beast. And figure a way to get it to come into my house.

A woman in blue yoga pants and a black and blue tunic strode toward us, her eyes locked in our direction, her gaze darting between Dee and me.

"Let's go inside," I said to him. "I really need to fuck you. Fuck you so hard. Right, right now."

God, I was such a bitch. First, I freak him out. Then I dangle sex at the most wildly inappropriate moment.

Not that Dee was fool enough to believe me, though he certainly had been surprised by my words. Most of him had figured out now what I was doing. But part of him was also sort of willing.

That was good. Real desire pouring off him. Real fear pouring off me. I trusted Dee, but I was about to put my life in his hands, and only an idiot wouldn't have some trepidation. I had a giant bag of it.

We walked fast straight across the Strand, up the path to my porch and then inside. I shut the door but left it slightly ajar. Four bottles stood on the table in my foyer—two for klim, two for us for later.

I picked up the two meant for the klim.

"Get the others and come into the parlor," I said.

We needed the klim completely inside the house.

All the klim need do was push the door open and join us. All we had to do was make sure it did. I stood by the chaise looking through the bay window to the Strand wondering what else I could say to Dee to get an emotional rise.

His hands were on my chest suddenly, pushing me down on the chaise. I yelped in surprise. He started to fall on top of me but caught himself with his arms so that he loomed above me.

"Maybe I love you, too," he said. "What do you think about that?"

here was no time to sort out whether Dee was trying to generate new emotions, or meant what he'd said and if he did, how I might feel about that. The door slammed open.

The klim had thrown off its human disguise. It sped into the parlor and stood at the end of the sofa, standing on its hind legs, glaring down at us. The wart hog-like horns curving upwards from either side of its mouth dripped brown saliva. A smell like sewage radiated from it. Its bumpy, gray toadish skin seemed to gleam from some dark, internal light.

The klim roared and reached a horn-covered, four-fingered hand toward my throat. My heart galloped. Dee began chanting the spell that would send it back to the Brume. I joined in.

From the corner of my eye I saw Dee pull the stopper from his bottle. Mine had rolled between the cushions when he'd pushed me down on the chaise. I dug around madly trying to find it without taking my eyes off the klim. I didn't know if the liquid in Dee's bottle would be enough or if we needed the amount in both. Both, I reasoned, or we wouldn't have two bottles.

Dee dashed the elixir in the klim's face. The beast stepped back as if punched and roared again. It swiped its hand at Dee's head. He ducked away.

I found the second bottle. My hand closed around it and I pulled it from behind the cushion. I yanked the stopper free and splashed the elixir on the klim's face and chest. The beast screamed, its wail shrinking as it faded and then was gone.

I stared at the spot where it had been, barely believing we'd managed to send it back.

"Quick," Dee said. "We have to follow it."

My pulse thundered in my temples. I drew a breath and centered myself the way I might on the rink in the midst of a critical play. I fingered the red orb in my pocket, its magic zinging through me like electrical jolts. How was I going to hold the orb to close the rift if it hurt like that?

Dee handed me one of the two remaining vials of elixir. We drained both vials dry.

My ears popped, the same way they had at the ice rink and before my vision of the Brume. Multicolored sparks filled the room. The eagle tattoo on my arm prickled and grew warm. Dee took my hand at the same moment that a flash of intense blue light burned my eyes. I squeezed them shut and held onto him. The sound of storm winds whooshed in my ears, but there was no brush of air on my skin.

"Oona." Dee's voice was urgent.

I opened my eyes. The Brume stretched out around us, a sulfurous desert with high, jagged hills in the distance. This wasn't where I'd entered before. There was no wall, no river of red molten liquid. I had no way to judge how near or far to the rift we were.

The acrid air was as yellow as the sand—a jaundiced

world. I scanned the land and the sky. Nothing crawled, slithered, ran, or flew that I could see. No wind blew. The silence was the stillness of a vacuum. It made my skin crawl.

Dee elbowed me lightly and jutted his chin in sign for me to look where his gaze was focused. The membrane. We'd landed well away and had a walk ahead of us. Once we reached the membrane, we'd still need to find the rift.

"Where did you send the klim?" My words seemed swallowed by the silence.

"As far from the membrane as I could," Dee said, striding off.

I rushed to keep up. "So, we won't have to worry about it?"

Dee shrugged. "Who knows what magic the klim has."

"So, worry about it," I said, "and maybe about other creatures, too."

"It's a dark world," he said, and quickened his pace. "Full of dark things."

"Yeah," I said, my throat going dry again. "I've seen some of them."

Dee must have heard the scratch in my voice. He reached into a front pocket of his cargo shorts and pulled out an old-fashioned flask—silver, with runes inscribed on it and curved to lie discretely against a body.

"Water," he said as he handed it to me.

I drank as I walked. The water was warm but wet. It soothed my throat.

"Thanks," I said and handed it back.

Dee took a swig and stowed the flask back in his pocket. I wondered what other things were tucked away in those pockets, things he thought we might need, magical things.

My legs were beginning to tire by the time the diaphanous membrane loomed in front of us, a translucent fence reaching toward the sky. Except—I realized—the fence curved inward toward the top. I craned my neck to look skyward. Not a fence at all. A dome. A way to keep in things that flew.

Not that it made any difference. Fence or dome, as long as the rift remained, the chance of more things from this world coming into ours remained too.

Since we'd come into the Brume, the only sounds had been our words and the breadcrumb crunch of the sand beneath our feet. I cringed when a long, low whistle sounded behind us. I swung around and looked back but saw only the seemingly endless stretch of yellow desert and yellow sky.

"Did you hear that?" I said quietly.

Dee didn't speak, only nodded.

Something was out there, behind our backs. The skin on my neck prickled. I started to speak again, but Dee shot me a warning look. I kept my thoughts to myself. There was nothing we could do anyway. If something was hunting us— and something definitely was—we'd have to wait until it got closer to deal with it.

If we could deal with it.

The fresh eagle and sunrays tattoo on my upper arm tingled, almost as if assuring me it would do the best job it could. Magic ink or not, we were vulnerable. I'd be stupid to forget that.

As if I could forget. The whistle tore through the air again, still behind us but closer now. I looked all around but couldn't see anything. What if whatever was approaching was invisible to our eyes? It could come right down on our heads before we knew it.

Dee seemed almost to not have heard the whistle. He had, though. I saw it in the slight tensing of his shoulders. Felt it in the sudden shift of attention in his mind. He didn't let the whistle distract him. Goalie focus—calm but ready.

Lessons I'd learned on the rink flooded through my mind. *Anticipate without panic. See the whole field of play. Know what you're going to do next, and next after that, before you make your move.* Actions that led to victory. I exhaled slowly, releasing my tension and worry as best I could.

Focus. Victory was all about focus.

I'd touched the membrane in my vision of the Brume. I touched it now. It felt softer than it had before. Did that mean it was thinner now and would be easier to breach, or more elastic and harder to pierce? Hard to anticipate your next move when you didn't have much history to draw on.

Focus.

I kept my palm on the membrane as we moved forward, feeling, as well as looking, for any small tears I might have missed before.

A clicking noise sounded behind us. When I turned to look for the source of the sound, my fingers slipped into a small hole in the membrane.

"Dee," I said wanting to tell him about the tear I'd found. And about the spider-looking thing the size of a Saint Bernard hurtling toward us, its eight eyes focused on me, its front pinchers held up and clicking like castanets.

Dee glanced at me and then over my shoulder.

"Listen," he said and tapped his hand against his head.

I tuned into him. His mind was racing, flipping between how to deal with the spider-thing and sending me the words to the spell to close the hole—the one he'd memorized at Sudie's. I pulled the orb from my pocket and hoped to hell it would work. The orb sent an electric jolt of magic zinging through my hand and up my arm, but I held on to it.

I felt a new tension in Dee and turned my head to see what he was seeing. Yellow dust rising across the sulfur-sand desert.

Beasts. The word blasted from his mind. *Hurry, Oona.*

This wasn't even the main rift. How many other holes and tears did we need to close to heal the membrane? Were there things here, small but evil, that could fit through a hole this size?

I sorted through Dee's thoughts and focused on the spell words. I rubbed the orb over the hole and intoned the healing spell Dee was sending.

I hardly registered the sound of Dee's speaking voice— spell words completely different from the ones I needed to say. A sizzling sound and a high-pitched wail rose behind me, but I didn't look. Not until the hole was closed and smooth under my palm.

"Thank you," a voice—a strange watery sound—whispered in my head

I stood, looking for the source of the words, but saw nothing. The spider thing was gone. A pile of ash lay where it had stood.

Dee ran his hands across his hair, pushing it back from his face.

The dust devil stirring the sand had grown larger. And closer. Dee gave my shoulder a little shove and broke into a run.

"Slow down," I said, wishing he could read my mind like I read his. So much faster and easier than words. "Slow. Down. I need to feel for small tears."

He slowed, but I felt his tension ratchet up.

Forget the damn holes, he thought. *Find the main rift and fix it before that fucking thing coming across the desert reaches us.*

The watery voice whispered in my head again. "No more holes but the one."

179

The membrane. The membrane was alive and sentient. The small tear had pained it, but the rift pained it more.

I broke into a run, blessing hockey for giving me endurance.

Even so, I was breathing hard by the time I spotted the place where the membrane was torn. And the hole. Bigger now than when I'd been here before. More ragged. Gaping.

I glanced across the desert. The swirling sand was closer —close enough to see small clumps of sand rising and falling. The ink on my arm tingled, warning me of danger, ramping up its power to give what protection it could. I felt Dee center himself and focus on the sand cloud. I didn't know if something was in the cloud or it was the sand itself we needed to worry about. Not that it mattered. Judging from the controlled tension roiling off Dee, we needed to be plenty worried in general.

I knelt beside the rift. I wanted Dee to slip across back to our world now, before I closed the hole, but knew he wouldn't. No more than I would. We wouldn't abandon the other.

Dee was again chanting a spell out loud while thinking the enchantment to close the rift. I had to concentrate hard to separate the spoken and thought words, since both were going on in his thoughts. I found the part of his mind focused on the healing spell but only listened enough to be sure I was right. I'd got the spell now. I knew it by heart. I chanted low and rubbed the orb over the ragged edges of the rift.

The sand cloud was close enough now that I could see into it.

"The klim told them all," the watery voice said. "Told about the rift, the easy prey on the other side the klim had devoured. Cloud rolled for days to get here, to burst through, to destroy what contains it. Other creatures come too, seeking to destroy me, seeking the way across. You and the wizard must save me."

I saw them, the other creatures. They came walking on two, four, and six legs across the sand. They came scuttling and slithering and flying. I rubbed the orb over the edges of the rift. It was closing but slowly. Too slowly.

"Hurry," said the watery voice.

The cloud was nearly on Dee. I'd learned the healing spell but stayed in his head. I heard him intoning spells to turn back the cloud. Saw the cloud halt, spinning in place. Felt it trying to decide what to do next.

Dee had pulled a silver ball the size of a newborn's fist from his pocket. It lay in his outstretched palm, white light pulsating from it. Light emanated from him, too, crazy purple light bathing him in its glow. His voice was strong, intoning the spells that held back the sand cloud and the stalking beasts. I turned my attention back to the rift.

"*Jetoh de bycon freedsa,*" I said under my breath. The orb sliding on the torn membrane made a small shooshing sound. The air was hot and still. Perspiration rolled slowly down my sides.

Step it up, Oona, I heard in my head and looked Dee's way. The light from the silver ball was fading, its power running out. The eagle on my arm tingled and prickled. Maybe its protection was running out too. What good was magic that had a time limit?

A great blast of fury from the sand cloud rolled through my mind. The cloud didn't have thoughts the way humans did, only basic emotions that roiled in it like the churning waves of a turbulent sea. Waves sought the shore. The cloud sought the rift. In its wake lay scattered bits of beasts and beastlets that had stood in its way.

We stood in its way.

Dee turned to face it and stretched out his right arm. A great pulse of energy that I saw like a blinding purple light, shot from his palm. The cloud hesitated, spinning on itself in place, then rushed forward again.

The cloud seemed stronger now, as if it had nourished itself on the energy sent to stop it. If the cloud ate magic, grew stronger on power, how could we stop it?

I jammed into Dee's mind. He'd seen the same thing I had, drawn the same conclusion. His magic was useless against the cloud. Worse than useless—it made the cloud more violent.

Dee reached into his pocket and drew out something small enough to fit in his closed fist. He drew a deep breath, then ran toward the cloud.

"No!" I yelled.

Dee and the cloud collided, dirt and sand spewing into the air. The cloud spun faster, expanding until it covered him completely and he was lost from my sight. I heard screams. Dee's. I felt for his thoughts but found nothing.

"No," I shouted again. I jumped to my feet, all instinct, fury, and determination, and ran toward the sand cloud. The sigil on my arm burned. Energy and power burst through me.

From the corner of my eye, I saw things that ran, crawled, slithered, and flew racing toward the rift. My mind spun. Of course. Of course. If Dee and I both left the rift, the things would see their chance and take it. Most of the beasts were too big; they'd never fit through the rift still not mended. But there were four or five small things, tiny enough to slide into our world. Small things but mean. I felt their malevolence like bites to my soul.

I stopped, frozen in place. Save Dee or mend the last of the rift and keep the evil in the Brume?

I whirled back to the membrane and channeled the intense

energy roiling through me into the orb, willing it to work faster, to close the rift before the beasts could get through.

It seemed to take forever. The orb was hot in my hand. Burning. There was only a tiny speck left to close. I rubbed the orb over the last bit and the rift sealed shut. The membrane sighed.

I pulled to my feet and turned. The sand cloud was gone, and Dee with it. My heart clenched.

The demon-beasts howled with rage and turned to attack their neighbors, as if they needed some way—any way—to vent their frustration. My heart pounded. Sweat trickled down my sides. Dee was gone, and I had no way out of this place.

Almost as one, the beasts stopped attacking each other and noticed me again. Fear rooted me to the spot. Even if I could make my legs run, there was no place to go.

Then the klim was there—suddenly—only feet away. *"Who knows what magic the klim has,"* Dee had said. This magic at least—to travel from wherever Dee had sent it and be here now.

I stood alone, my back against the membrane.

The klim grinned its wart-hog smile and leapt at my throat.

*T*ime seemed to slow. The klim leaned toward me in infinite increments, its warty gray arms outstretched, its black, horn-covered hands reaching toward my throat. Dark energy poured from the beast, cascading over me like dirty water.

My heartbeat seemed to slow, too, which was weird considering how terrified I was. Focus, I told myself. Focus. Watch the hands but also watch the chest; hands can wave everywhere but the beast will move in the direction its chest points. Don't get fooled.

Don't think about Diego.

Oh my God. Dee.

Focus.

The eagle on my arm tingled and pulsed. Energy burst inside me, spreading from my chest out through my arms, down my legs, up to the top of my head. I swept the klim's meaty arm away as if it were nothing more than a twig.

The beast roared its rage. It swiped toward me again. I crouched and pushed off with my legs, propelling myself forward, my body angled so my shoulder landed dead center of the klim's chest. The beast stumbled, wobbling back a few steps on shaky legs.

These are things you learn on the rink: make use of distance. Lead into a collision with your shoulder. Bend your knees to lower your center of gravity. Know what you're going to do next but be ready to change your plan.

I used that distance, launching myself forward again and slamming hard into the klim. The beast fell. I fell on top of it and grabbed for its throat.

I was fast but the klim was faster. Claws extended from the tips of the klim's horn-covered hands. I jerked back as its nails raked across my throat. Panic made my belly feel like it was filled with ice, but no blood dripped from where the klim had caught me. That was good.

If I didn't want to wind up with my throat slit like Brad Keel, I couldn't give the klim a second swipe at me. I grabbed for its arms, to pin them down.

The beast twisted its body, throwing me off. I hit the marshy ground on my back, the give of the soil lessening the impact. The beast leapt for my throat, its maw open, and roaring as though declaring its win. Its breath smelled like rotted meat. My ears rang from its roar. I barely managed to roll away from its reach. I jumped to my feet before the klim could catch me on the ground again.

Other beasts roared back at the klim. In my peripheral vision, legs moved restlessly, and feet stomped as the beasts ached to join in. Something cold and wet licked across my back, sending shivers up my spine.

In that moment of distraction, the klim closed a hand around my ankle and I tumbled down again.

The beast half-lifted itself, half-plunged forward and landed on top of me. Its arms clamped around my body, pinning my arms to my sides. The klim squeezed, pushing the air from my lungs. Its eyes glittered.

My tattoo burned. Magic, energy, and will screamed in my blood. I pushed my arms hard out to the sides, breaking the klim's hold. The moment I was free, I leapt back to my feet and shoved my boot-shod foot hard into the klim's throat. It grabbed my ankle again and pulled. I fell over hard on ground so marshy, that as I sank, the soil seemed to try to close around me.

The klim levered up and over me, pressing its fist in the hollow of my throat, pushing my head deeper into the ground. I choked and gagged. The klim grinned its wart-hog grin. Black energy poured off it like jets of steam.

Desperate energy poured into my mind and muscles. Now was the moment. If I couldn't stop the beast with this effort, I didn't know if I'd have the strength to try again. I grabbed the klim's arm in both my hands and flipped the beast onto its back on the ground. I struggled out of the marsh to my feet and dropped down on the klim's chest. Surprise and anger were in its eyes.

Now was the moment. Now, or maybe never. I didn't hesitate.

I clamped my hands on both sides of the klim's head and twisted hard and fast. The sound of cracking bone seemed to fill the Brume.

And then silence, as if all the creatures of the Brume had died with the klim.

I stood, breathing hard. Sweat covered my skin. The klim lay dead beneath me.

The silence broke in a cacophony of wild sounds. Beasts that had watched the struggle hissed and growled as they moved toward me—an army of things that slithered, flew, or bolted forward on any number of legs, their eyes glinting with frenzy. Things with teeth and claws. Things of hunger and rage.

The rift was closed. I had nowhere to run even if I had the strength. Every muscle in me ached. I couldn't fight them all off.

"Dee," I screamed as I came to my feet, wanting his name to be my last word, my final battle cry. I closed my hands into fists and leaped toward the closest beast.

Blue light filled my eyes, nearly blinding me. Wind whipped my hair and chilled my skin. I felt myself falling, falling . . .

When I hit bottom, I lay on my side on the floor in my parlor, panting hard. My throat ached where the klim had tried to strangle me.

Dee reached out a hand to help me up. I blinked up at him, unsure if he were real or something my mind conjured to comfort me in my last seconds.

"You're home, Oona," he said. "You're safe."

I *felt* the truth of his words.

I took his hand but only pulled myself into a sit. My heart felt ready to burst through my chest. Every muscle in my body cried out in pain. My throat seemed as dry as a lake on the moon. I licked my lips and said, "You're alive." And then, "Water."

He grinned an acknowledgment, reached into a pocket, and handed me the same container we'd shared in the Brume. I drank deeply and handed it back with a shaky hand.

"Is the rift still closed?" I said, desperation clear in my voice.

Dee nodded. "Sealed up tight. You did a fantastic job on that."

"Are you sure?" I said.

"Yes," he said. "I checked it on the way out."

It was an audacious statement. Checked it *how*? But the only vibe radiating off him was a bit of annoyance that I'd questioned his word. He'd checked. The rift was closed. That was that.

"How did you get us home?" I said. "The cloud carried you off. I was terrified for you." My voice dropped to a whisper. "I heard you scream. I thought the cloud had killed you."

He sank down to the floor next to me. "I guess I'm hard to kill. As hard to kill as you are. And, I had a little extra up my sleeve." He paused. "You didn't feel anything special from your new ink?"

The water had helped. Being back in my house helped. Dee being alive definitely helped. My brain still felt a little worn out and fuzzy, but bit by bit I was becoming myself again.

"I felt it tingling. Sort of telling me it was there and would do its best to protect me. When I fought the klim, it burned like fire."

I looked at him and swallowed hard. "I killed it, Dee. Broke its neck. I ..." Words stuck in my throat. I had no idea how to speak the emotions running through me. My pleasure and pride at having bested the klim. My horror that I'd killed a living, sentient being and was glad about it. I wasn't sorry I'd done it but was sad it had been necessary. I was more than a little surprised I'd been capable of it. Survival is a powerful motivator.

"The tingle is the sign that the tat is armed and ready," he said, not letting me dwell on the death. "That ink gives more than a bit of protection."

I waited for him to go on.

"The Gate mixed the inks personally and specially," he said. "Every time you felt the tingle, the magic in the ink flooded into you. Whatever magic you or I brought into the

Brume was intensified and multiplied." He paused again. "You didn't notice you could do things today that you couldn't yesterday?"

I thought about that. "You gave me the healing spell once, and I knew it by heart. I knew the sand cloud's emotions." I thought more about the question. Better to think about that than the klim. "More than abstract knowing, though. It was like being powered by the cloud's emotions, but they were turned around." I shook my head. "That's not quite right." I tried again. "The cloud's negative emotions enhanced positive power in me and helped me close the rift. When the klim attacked me, its negative emotions gave me the strength I needed to defeat it."

"That's exactly what happened," he said. "When the cloud grabbed me, every raging, furious emotion it had while we battled charged my personal power. It was pretty heady stuff."

"The power?"

"Yeah," Dee said. "I'm strong, but I swear, Oona, once the cloud had me and poured all its anger and hatred my way, I was invincible."

"Still?"

He shook his head. "I don't know. I don't think so. I wouldn't mind keeping that kind of power."

I pulled off my hoodie and touched the eagle on my upper arm. Having negative emotions affect me positively seemed terrific on the surface—it would make being in public a lot easier—but in my experience, great gifts tended to come with consequences.

He touched the place on his chest near his heart where the numeral one embraced by a crescent moon lay. "I'm pretty sure The Gate did this on purpose."

"Gave us magical ink?"

"I thought he'd probably do that, though it wasn't promised, and you never know with him. The Gate purposefully had us take the other's symbol into the Brume. The ink converted the cloud's dark emotions into power for me. Ink in a tat that not only symbolized you but was designed by you. Basically, symbolically, you saved my life."

That was a little too much to contemplate at the moment. I levered myself up to my feet. "You want a beer? I could use one."

Dee followed me into the kitchen. I pulled two Tecates and a bowl of limes from the fridge, popped my beer open and set the other on the table in the spot where he usually sat.

"Why would The Gate do that with the tats?" I said.

He settled in the chair and popped open his can. "The Gate would tell you that I don't always play well with others."

I scoffed. "You play a team sport at a level where it's all about being a team player, not an individual. Can't get much more 'plays well with others' than that."

"Goalie," he said and shrugged. "All by myself back there in net, waiting to make that big, spectacular save."

"Are you saying The Gate set this whole thing up as some sort of 'learn to be a team player' exercise for you?"

Dee took a deep swallow of beer and set the can on the table. "Hardly. He's not that big an asshole. Or that powerful. But he's not one to let an opportunity go by either."

I took another swallow of beer, my mind churning, slipping into rehashing all that had happened in the Brume. The crack of the klim's bones.

Dee leaned forward and stroked my cheek softly. "There were lessons for you in the Brume too."

I caught his hand against my cheek and held it there, needing that human touch.

He left his hand there a long moment before moving it away.

"I like working alone," he said. "You do too, but for a whole other reason. I don't want to be responsible for anyone but myself. You don't want anyone close to you for fear of what you'll feel from them, what they might want from you. Knowing The Gate, he saw this as an opportunity for us both to learn something. He tends to be that way."

He upended the can and finished what was left inside. He got up, put the empty can in the recycling bin, and sat back down. It struck me that we'd become mighty comfortable and casual around the other in a very short time.

"The thing is," Dee said, "we work well together. Two weeks ago, we didn't know each other. Since meeting, we've solved several murders and stopped anything else from coming over from the Brume into our world. Neither of us could have done it alone. It's kind of impressive."

I tilted my head in agreement. We did seem to be a good pairing in a lot of ways. We got along and were comfortable together. We trusted each other. We had sort of saved the world together. We definitely fit together in bed. So why did my stomach clench at the *couple* vibe he was giving off?

"If my sign saved your life, does it work out that your sign saved mine?" I said.

He nodded. "Once The Gate knew we were going into the Brume together, he would have done his best to make sure we both came out alive. Your sigil on me. Mine on you. Team play plus magic ink equals mutual salvation."

I sipped at my beer. "Thank him for that the next time you see him."

Dee smiled. "I will."

Exhaustion settled on me suddenly. I wanted a meal, a shower, and a very long sleep. Alone.

Dee sighed and closed his eyes—as worn out as I was and wanting the same things I did. Except he wanted to stay here tonight. Not to keep me safe, I didn't need his protection anymore—but because he liked my company. My human touch. I had to decide if I wanted to invite him or not.

These conflicted emotions were getting tiresome. Time to make a decision.

Tonight, choice meant picking between a warm body to curl next to, and my whole bed to myself. Choosing a friendly face in the morning, or peaceful solitude to start the day. A man who could actually cook breakfast, or a meal I made myself, for myself, without having to ask if he liked pepper in his eggs.

Dee offered someone who knew exactly how horrific this time had been and had shared the terrors of today. A lover I didn't have to hide my abilities from and who encouraged me to greater strength. A man I liked a lot and could be myself with. Someone who would have my back and would let me have his.

A partner.

The idea was growing on me.

Thank you for reading this book. I would be most grateful if you'd take a moment to leave a review on Amazon and Goodreads. Thank you.

Oona's adventures continue in *Barbed Wire Heart*. Click her to get your copy. mybook.to/BWH

AUTHOR'S NOTE

My very first favorite book when I was a kid was an illustrated version of *The Arabian Nights*. I loved those stories, especially "The Singing Tree," which is not one of the more famous ones but had a huge influence on me. The next book I fell in love with was Madeleine L'Engle's *A Wrinkle in Time*. You can see where this is going—science fiction, fantasy, and the idea of magic in the everyday world grabbed me early and never let go.

As I grew older, mysteries caught my attention. I loved Agatha Christie and Dorothy L. Sayers. Later I loved Martin Cruz Smith and Adrian McKinty. There was something very reassuring about those stories: the world and life may fall to pieces but in the end all will be put if not right, at least right-ish.

So, it's a little surprising it took me so long to combine murder mysteries and magic together in a story. And hockey. I love playing hockey and yet had never written characters that also played the game.

With *Ice-Cold Death,* I finally mashed all my favorite things together. The result is in your hands. I very much hope you enjoyed it.

Would you do me a favor? If you loved this book, thought it was meh, or even if you hated it would you be so kind as to leave a short review on Amazon? Your comments will help other readers decide if this might be something they'd like to dive into.

Ice-Cold Death is the first story in the projected five book Oona Goodlight series. If you'd like to know when future books in the series are available please join my VIP Readers here: VIP Readers, or meet and discuss with other readers in my Facebook group Alexes Razevich Readers and Friends.

Thank you for reading.
    ~Alexes Razevich

Book Three: *By the Shining Sea*

Contemporary Fantasy

Shadowline Drift – A psychological thriller with science fiction and fantasy elements. Perfect for fans of Inception or Lost.

ACKNOWLEDGMENTS

Many thanks to Dan McNeil, Richard Casey, and my amazing editor, Christina Frey, for their help in shaping this story.

Much love to Colin, Larkin, and Chris Razevich—I love you to the moon and stars and beyond.

Cover design by Deranged Doctor Design

ABOUT THE AUTHOR

Alexes Razevich writes speculative fiction with an emphasis on urban fantasy. She attended California State University San Francisco where she earned a degree in Creative Writing. After a successful career on the fringe of the electronics industry, including stints as Director of Marketing for a major trade show management company and as an editor for Electronic Engineering Times, she returned to her first love — fiction. She lives in Southern California with her husband and rescue dog, Rebel. When she isn't writing, she can usually be found playing hockey or traveling somewhere she hasn't been before.

Email: LxsRaz@yahoo.com
News and Updates: VIP Readers
Website: http://www.alexesrazevich.com/

 twitter.com/lxsraz

 instagram.com/lxsraz

 bookbub.com/authors/AlexesRaevich

Made in the USA
Middletown, DE
13 June 2020

97418474R00120